Tides *Of The* Desert

Saga Of A Girl From The Coast To The Desert And Back

VIVEK N SHETTY

notionpress
.com

INDIA · SINGAPORE · MALAYSIA

*I could hear **Sukesh** crying out loud. I knew they were hitting him mercilessly. If only he could tell them the truth, they would let us go. This was the last thing I had expected for my family in this alien land. I just wished to go back to India. I've had enough of this place.*

"Oh... Is that blood? What is that oozing out of the door? Why can't I get up from the chair and see it? Have they tied me to this chair? Where's Saarika?" "No... No... Saarika, don't go there... Saarika, don't..."

*I could see **Sajidbhai** in the corner of the room. He was crying. Suddenly, the door opened, and **Amma** walked in. She was holding a stick in her hand. She walked straight at me and whack, she hit my face! I blacked out.*

*I opened my eyes, and **Saarika** was sleeping right next to me. There was no blood, no Sajidbhai, no Amma. Was I dreaming?*

I looked for my mobile to check the time. It was 2 am! Oh, God! I was dreaming. I had to go to court in the morning. I needed to get back to sleep. But somehow, I wasn't feeling sleepy. That was a bad dream, and I was wide awake. What's that smell? It smelled like paddy! The paddy from my home. Lush green paddy fields. Was it the harvest season? I had forgotten the harvest calendar since coming to this country. I wish I were back home.

Contents

Gratitude

*W*riting this book was not as easy as I had imagined; it took me two years to complete. Reading a book in just an hour or two is vastly different from writing one. This was a dream fuelled by my love for writing—something I needed to check off my bucket list before I kicked the bucket. I am deeply grateful to the **Almighty** for guiding me through this journey.

*Several individuals were instrumental in bringing this book to life, and I am deeply grateful to them. My **father**, who instilled in me a love of reading from a young age, supported this passion despite his meagre income. My **mother** would gently persuade my father whenever I longed for a comic book and threw a fuss.*

*My high school friend, **Rohith Bhat**, further fuelled my imagination by sharing his vast collection of comic books, many of which were unheard of in India at the time.*

*My wife, **Swapna**, was the first to read the manuscript. When she told me she couldn't put the book down once she started reading, it gave me the confidence to move forward.*

***Prathibha Sujith**, this book would not have been completed without you. The time and effort you devoted to correcting grammar like a schoolteacher, offering insights, rewriting sentences, refining sequences, and so much more have been invaluable. This book is as much yours as it is mine; I cannot thank you enough.*

*To a few of my **friends** who encouraged me after reading the draft, your support meant the world to me. To the **Notion Press** team, your persistence and guidance helped shape this book into reality.*

*And to you, **dear reader**, with a heart full of thanks, I welcome you. May this book be your companion, from the first word to the last whisper. Your support means everything to me.*

Wedding Bells and a Leap of Faith

Ultimately, the wedding concluded. It was nearly 3 in the afternoon. The large wedding hall, with its air conditioning humming gently until now, seemed to have shut down. That meant it was time for us to vacate the premises. The hall, which had a capacity of around 500 people, felt empty now, with only about 20 members from both families lingering about. The groom and bride had come down from the stage and mingled with family members. I glanced at the large stage area, which looked beautiful. It was splendidly decorated with colourful flowers, featuring a backdrop of white tulips alongside bright red flowers that I couldn't identify. In the centre was a beautifully ornate chair where the bride and groom were meant to sit. With the stage empty now, children were fighting for a place on the chair where the bride and groom had been sitting a few minutes ago. The two large brass lamps were still burning brightly on the edge of the stage, facing the audience. The floor on the stage was scattered with holy rice or Akshata[1], and the children kept skidding and falling over it. Bright lights focused on the stage suddenly turned off, rendering the stage a dull hue. The photographers were busily dashing about, capturing candid photographs. Oh, what a lovely feeling it was to be the centre of attention for a change, albeit for a short time, much like those celebrities pursued by the paparazzi. A few seniors were seated in the front row, engaged in conversation. Those who spoke to them were touching their feet to receive their blessings. Young girls and boys, adorned in glamour, were busily snapping selfies. Suddenly, someone called out my name, jolting me back to the present moment.

It was time for me, the bride, to bid a formal farewell to my family. All my relatives gathered around me after the bride and groom received blessings from all the elders. I hadn't felt any emotions until a lady began singing a mournful song about the girl, the bride, being sent off to her husband's home. She sang of how she had been raised like a princess in her home, and now that she was leaving for her husband's house, how she ought to be cared for, and so forth. I thought, what

---

1. Akshata: Unbroken rice dipped in turmeric or vermillion, dried and thrown over the heads of the bride and the groom as a form of blessing during wedding.

the...? Where did this lady come from? A perfectly joyous occasion suddenly turned to tears as everyone around wiped their eyes. My younger sister was wailing. I found myself in a state of confusion. Should I cry with everyone or merely smile and uplift their spirits? I wasn't ready for this. In less than a minute, it felt as though I were being sentenced to life imprisonment, and everyone around me was mourning it. Nevertheless, I played along, and we all made our way to the groom's car.

After all the goodbyes and wiping our tearful eyes, as newlyweds, we were to drive directly to my husband's family home from the wedding hall. My mother, my two sisters, and my brother-in-law accompanied me, while my two suitcases full of clothes followed in a different car. That was the custom. The bride's family would drop the newlywed bride at the groom's house, enjoy some refreshments provided by the groom's family, and then bid farewell, leaving the bride in her new home. This marked the beginning of a new phase in my life—fascinating! Dreamy! It was a new experience, perhaps a life-changing experience for the better. I had many dreams about how I would care for my husband and my in-laws, and how I would be in their good books.

Our car drove along the highway of the coastal town of Udupi for about thirty minutes before veering off onto a narrower asphalt road leading to my husband's village. We passed a few houses intermittently before the car took another turn and entered a muddy track. A canopy of trees soon covered the open sky as our car slowed to navigate the uneven road. My husband sat in the back seat beside me, appearing quite pleased as he stole glances at me. The driver, my husband's cousin, was chatting in the front seat with another cousin. I was more interested in our destination; after all, this would be my new home for the rest of my life. We traversed the forested area along the winding, muddy paths. The sun was already setting. Suddenly, the forest cleared to reveal a spacious open area, and I spotted a sizeable old Mangalore-tiled one-storey house. Areca nuts were spread across the veranda floor to dry in the sun. Our car was parked next to the veranda when two dogs came running, barking towards us, displaying all their aggression but quickly shifting to whimpers of submission and excitement as soon as they recognised the family members. They seemed rather apologetic for their earlier barking, I presumed.

I got out of the car with the heavy bridal dress and jewellery. The dogs approached me with apprehension and started sniffing when I heard my father-in-law shout at them. Off they ran, looking back at me. From one agricultural family to another, I instantly connected with the surroundings and the ecosystem. It didn't feel like a stranger's house, though it was. I was stepping here for the first time in my life. By the time I walked along the narrow mud path to the veranda and then to the elaborately carved wooden front door, my sisters-in-law were prepared with the *Arati* [2]. They waved the lit flame at us (the bride and groom) in a circular motion, applied *vermilion* [3] along the part of my hairline, and instructed me to enter the house with my right foot first.

It was a typical coastal house in Udupi: a brick structure with a slanted Mangalore-tiled roof. It was my mother's dream house, and it was much bigger and better than the house where I grew up.

Our house had a thatched roof and mud walls. The most remarkable aspect of these homes is that they remain warm during cold seasons and cooler in harsh summers. Cold

---

2.   Arati: A Hindu ritual in which light from a flame (fuelled by camphor, ghee, or oil) is ritually waved to venerate deities.
3.   Vermillion: Hindu women use vermilion along the hair parting line, known as sindoor, to signify that they are married.

weather was rare in my part of the world, but from November to January, the nights could be regarded as mildly chilly. Monsoons are exceptionally fierce in this region. But the thatched hut used to hold up to the fury of lord Varuna [4] most of the time. Sometimes, rainwater would leak in certain places, and we would have to borrow vessels from the kitchen to collect the water.

The problem with these roofs was that they had to be periodically changed as the straw would become brittle over time. That was why getting a Mangalore tiled [5] roof was a dream for every thatched roof house owner, and my parents were no exception.

The house had an open veranda, where most of us would spend time resting, chatting and in summer, men would even sleep here. It was a favourite place of resting for my grandfather, who, in his old age, spent a significant part of the day chewing on betelnuts, idling and

---

4.   Varuna: Hindu God, associated with the sky, oceans and water.
5.   Mangalore Tile: Rectangular tiles made of laterite clay and placed as roofing interconnected at 45 degrees.

sleeping there. These were the days before mobiles and the Internet. After an early dinner, the family would gather there to discuss various topics. There was humour, gossip, arguments, emotion, devotion, singing, storytelling, and more. There was a strong sense of bonding among all family members. Fast forward to the current scenario; ironically, after the advent of the internet and mobile phones, we are superficially connected to the world yet disconnected from our family members. Each individual is immersed in their respective mobile phone in different parts of the house.

This transition was gradual, however. During the pre-electricity days, dinner was served at 7 p.m.; by 8:30 p.m., everyone was asleep. Once electricity arrived in our house, we began reading magazines and newspapers after dinner. Later, we stopped reading, imagining, and dreaming when the television came along. We began watching someone else's imagination, relegating our dreams to the backseat. But at least we used to spend time together. That ended with the arrival of smartphones.

Beyond the veranda lay a small hall, two tiny rooms, and a kitchen. All rooms were quite small compared to those found in modern Indian homes. To provide some perspective, the entire house could comfortably fit within an area of 600 square feet.

There was a large yard in front of the house where the paddy was threshed and the grains separated post-harvest season. The cattle shed was right opposite the house, with the yard separating them. In rural India, cattle are an integral part of the village ecosystem. We had buffaloes used for tilling the paddy fields and cows for producing milk, of which a small portion was used for our consumption, and the rest sold to the village's Cooperative dairy. During my growing-up years, six people lived in this house apart from me, my grandfather, my parents and my two siblings. By the time I was born, my uncles had separated from the joint family and my grandmother had passed away.

In contrast, my husband's house had solid brick walls and a *Mangalore-tiled* roof. There was something called *Upparige*, or a floor above the ground floor, which could be accessed through stairs inside the house. There were areca and coconut trees all around. The house overlooked paddy fields beyond the veranda, which appeared ready for harvest. The evening sun cast a golden hue all around. In the corner of the veranda, there was a well. A *Tulsi* [6] plant grew like a bonsai and appeared quite old. I could also see the cow shed a short distance from the main house. There were roosters, a hen with her chicks pecking at the soft earth, two cats lounging about, and two dogs strolling around majestically, indifferent to anyone nearby. The chirping of the birds sounded remarkably loud against the stillness of the surroundings. Overall, it was a delightful place. I took an instant liking to it.

There were many guests about. My sisters-in-law were present throughout the house asserting their authority, while their husbands and friends from Mumbai joked in broken *Hindi* [7] with a pronounced South Indian accent. I sat in a corner chair, more interested in viewing the paddy fields through the bars of the large window in the hall.

---

6.   Tulsi Plant: Basil or Holy Basil
7.   Hindi: Language of India predominantly spoken in the mid and northern parts of India.

Suddenly, my attention was drawn by the eldest sister of my husband, Sukesh. "Come on, bride, let's see how good a cup of tea you can make. Let's have a round of tea for all."

I got up and headed straight to the unfamiliar kitchen. In the meantime, my mother-in-law entered and said, "Let me help you, dear."

She must be in her late 60s, a bit frail, with not much fat on her body. This is typical of members of agricultural families, given their daily hard labour. She wore a simple saree even to the wedding, and she was still wearing the same outfit. Slightly bent, but she had a pleasant face. With a smile and a big round red *Bindi* [8] on her forehead, she radiated warmth. She looked like someone who played a subdued role all her life, playing second fiddle to the demands of her husband and children. In helping me out, she ended up preparing the tea herself. I had a strange liking for her as I was dreading that I would get a strict mother-in-law. I poured the tea into the cups and took it out to serve all those present and chatting in the living room hall.

---

8. Bindi: A round shaped vermillion mark worn in the middle of the forehead by Indian women, especially Hindus.

"Ohhh… tastes like Amma's tea," said the second sister to the loud laughter of all the guests around. I smiled meekly. So did my amma sitting at the other corner. She passed a helpless glance at me.

The groom's family threw a few more taunts at my family members. No marriage is complete without it, I guess. When my family members were about to leave, the sister-in-law's gang of three said, seemingly joking, "Who is going to remove all her bridal stuff?". I could see my Amma and sisters looking at each other's faces. I was about to say I would do it myself and ask them to leave. But it was hardly an hour since I had entered this house. I didn't want to sound rude or give any scope for misunderstanding on the first day. My people had no choice but to stay back and remove all the accessories from my hair, makeup, etc. They left after almost an hour.

The day stretched deep into the night. Our wedding night. I felt butterflies fluttering in my stomach. I was both nervous and excited. I had never had any boyfriends in my life. I had never experienced anything remotely sexual. Sukesh was looking at me from across the room with a cheeky smile. I fixed my gaze on his and blushed, struggling to conceal it from the inquisitive eyes of my sisters-in-law.

After dinner, we all sat on the veranda, ready to go to bed after an exhausting day, when my father-in-law said, "Tonight is a lunar eclipse, so it's advisable for the bride and groom to sleep separately." This elicited giggles from my sisters-in-law, who seemed to oddly enjoy this twist of events. There goes my wedding night. Sukesh didn't protest; he simply gave me a look of despair and went to sleep in the living room. Meanwhile, I went inside and lay down on the flower-adorned bed, all by myself.

Post-wedding, it is customary for the newly married couple to visit various temples nearby. The relatives who lived nearby also invited the newlyweds to their homes for lunch or dinner. The second and third night we spent at a relative's house. I was not even able to talk to Sukesh alone. We didn't get the "We-Time". The fourth night, we were in Sukesh's father's ancestral house. There was a *Pooja*[9] scheduled there for the village deity. It was also one of Sukesh's brother-in-law's birthday. They insisted on us staying back. But by

9.   Pooja: The act of worship. Especially in religions like Hinduism, where idol worship is predominant.

this point, Sukesh was growing impatient as well. He insisted that we would go back home. I could sense his deep frustration. I smiled inwardly. After dinner, he nearly dragged me into the car, bypassing all the relatives, and we drove home. It was a thirty-minute drive during which he held my hand the entire time. I began to sweat. My heart raced. I looked at him and he fixed his intense gaze on me. A shiver ran down my spine, enhanced by the cool breeze from the car's open window.

We reached home and Sukesh was in such a hurry that he locked the house's main door and carried me to the bedroom. I was laughing nervously.

Exhausted as we were, we had no idea when we fell asleep. Around one in the night, we heard someone knocking on the door. It was raining heavily outside. Sukesh went to open the main door of the house and spoke to someone. I was not in the mood to get up from the bed. But I was concerned about who and what emergency it could be at this time of the night. Sukesh came in hurriedly and started dressing up to go out.

"What happened?" I sat up on the bed with the sheets drawn over my naked body.

"Prabha (his youngest sister), her husband and Sada (his cousin's son) have met with an accident. I'm going to the hospital now. You sleep. They say they are not in danger. I'll call you in the morning." And he rushed out of the house, leaving me alone in the big, unfamiliar house.

I couldn't sleep the whole night. Early in the morning, Sukesh called up. Unfortunately, the boy, Sada, succumbed to his injuries in the night. I was very nervous. Nervous that the blame would fall on me as the new bride and the bearer of bad luck. Sukesh consoled me, saying it was a freak accident and nobody would blame it on my luck. Fortunately, the other family members also concurred with Sukesh. Perhaps they had a few alcoholic drinks and drove late at night; moreover, the rain may have also impaired visibility, said Sukesh.

Rewind Mode – Courtship

India predominantly believes in arranged marriages, a concept that the Western world is often suspicious of due to a lack of understanding. Like any other girl of marriageable age, I received numerous proposals from prospective grooms. However, I was hesitant to marry because of the situation at home. I was now the sole earning member. If I married, all financial responsibilities would fall upon my mother and younger sister. I was unprepared to place this burden on their shoulders—not yet. This dulled the allure of marriage, leading me to refuse many proposals. Eventually, one of our relatives, who usually arranged proposals for us, gave me an ultimatum. He said, "If you refuse this man, I will stop getting any other marriage proposals for you."

This left me grappling with a tough decision. The custom was for the prospective groom and his family to meet the girl and her family at a temple. Both parties would see and converse with one another, and the bride and groom would also speak privately. If all conditions were met and both the man and woman were agreeable, the next step of engagement and marriage would follow.

I reluctantly agreed and went alone to the temple in the nearby town of Kapu, where my elder sister and her husband were supposed to meet me. Throughout the bus journey, I cried, anxious about my mother and sister. Who would look after them after I married? I wasn't ready for this marriage until my younger sister had completed her studies and secured a job. My Amma persuaded me to go and meet the man. She promised not to pressure me into marriage if I didn't like him. That was our agreement.

I wore one of my mother's nicer sarees[10]. She had a few sarees that her brother and my father had got her. These were carefully preserved and worn only on special occasions. As it was summer, the saree felt uncomfortable to wear. A string of jasmine adorned my braided hair. I was all dressed up for the "marriage interview."

I was slim and dark-complexioned, standing at 5'5". I didn't consider myself as pretty as my sisters. I was the family's tomboy, convinced I was the protector of the three women—at least, that was my thought. I was

---

10. Saree (Sari): A garment consisting of a length of cotton or silk elaborately draped around the body, traditionally worn by women in India.

sandwiched between the first and last child. Do you know what a middle child must endure? The elder sibling is the firstborn and, therefore, privileged, while the younger one is pampered. As the middle child, I was neither privileged nor pampered. A raw deal. That said, I possessed the maturity to overcome these feelings at a young age. My love for my parents and siblings never wavered despite this difference in treatment. We were one solid, strong unit. Even to this day, I pray to God to keep my mother and siblings safe, bearing any problems in their lives myself and not letting them bear the burden.

When I came to my senses, I had reached my destination, where my elder sister and her husband were waiting for me. I disembarked from the bus and walked to the temple with them. Inside the temple complex, we made the customary offerings to the deity. The ancient temple was constructed from solid granite, which was abundant locally. The interior of the temple complex was pleasantly cool, thanks to the granite's low heat conductivity, so we lingered inside for a while. No one was around except for a few devotees and two priests going about their daily routine. Occasionally, the sound of the temple bell would ring out. We noticed an old man sitting in another corner, who we later realised was the prospective groom's father. After some time, we saw two men enter the temple. We speculated it might be the would-be groom. After the customary prayer to the deity, they approached us. Indeed, it was the prospective groom, his father, and a friend of the groom's.

After exchanging pleasantries and introducing everyone present, it was time for the would-be couple to chat privately, away from all the family members. He was well-built, or slightly on the plumper side, standing around 5' 9" in height, with a wheatish complexion, lightly bearded, and curly hair. With a mild smile, he wore a dark blue striped shirt neatly tucked into grey trousers. I could easily pass him off as a good-looking chap. However, I was not willing to "fall" for him. I was in a state of confusion. The woman in me was attracted to him, but the situation back home did not allow my mind to say yes. Reluctantly, I spoke to him. Although I approached him with resentment, he charmed me with the way he spoke. I was honest with him about the financial situation at my home. It wasn't good.

Although agriculture was my family's primary occupation, we lacked a steady source of cash income. The only way to earn money was by selling surplus paddy or rice and cow's milk to the local milk cooperative. However, this income was barely enough to support our family of six. We struggled to make ends meet each month, with little left for groceries, repairs, or even small indulgences—luxuries were a distant dream. Every rupee mattered. We lived in a village in South India.

My village is still somehow frozen in time. People outside its boundaries find it hard to imagine our village and its lifestyle. They find it hard to believe that such a village exists today. You, too, may doubt if my village is situated in a 20th- or 21st-century context. That's how calm and serene my village was/ is.

Now imagine this: a drone shot capturing a verdant landscape from above, acres adorned in various hues of lush green, delicate paddy fields. You can see multiple shades of green as the wind caresses the fragile paddy saplings, creating patterns of waves. Have you ever smelled the young paddy saplings? You should—it's a unique odour; rather, 'fragrance' would be a better word. Picture acres upon acres of such paddy fields. The essence of that scent lingers omnipresent in the surroundings. Now, can you see a thatched-roof house nestled in the midst of this greenery? That is my house, with a cow shed opposite it, separated by a courtyard in between. The girl sweeping the courtyard is my elder sister, Shalini. The old man resting on the narrow veranda is my maternal grandfather. My Amma is one of the many bent-over, saree-clad women you see in the paddy fields, transplanting the saplings into the wet slush of the field. You can also spot me emerging from the cow shed, carrying a steel jar filled with fresh, creamy milk. Yes, I have just milked one of the three cows we own. The youngest girl you see washing utensils in the backyard is my younger sister, Sharanya.

Now, turn your gaze to the edge of the greenery, around 500 metres away. You can also spot another similar thatched hut belonging to my Amma's cousins. My village is not just a typical cluster of houses seen in old Indian films. Here, we have scattered houses, each positioned some 500 metres to possibly a kilometre apart, separated by lush greenery. Beautiful, isn't it?

Bejjoli is the name of our village, situated in the Udupi District of southern coastal Karnataka, India. Do not Google it, as you will not find it. These paddy fields are our lifeline; this is where our staple diet of rice for the family and hay for the cattle originates. We cultivate our rice and vegetables, both for our consumption and to sell any surplus for some cash.

There is also this small forested area attached to most of the properties in the village, which in my mother tongue is called Paadi [11]. These Paadis feature both large and small trees.

---

11. Paadi: A small forested area next to the houses of the village earmarked for timber or gathering of dry leaves.

The larger trees are typically older specimens, such as teak and jackfruit, which are commonly used in building roofs for houses or for making furniture. A small variety of trees, known as 'karmar', can be found clustered in these Paadis. These trees generally reach heights of 6 to 10 feet and maybe around 6 inches in diameter; they serve two purposes. The stems and twigs are utilised as firewood, while the dried leaves that fall to the ground are collected and spread across the cowshed floor. These dry leaves help to keep the floor warm for the cattle. As cow dung and urine mix with the leaves, they create rich compost. No, it doesn't stagnate; there is a drainage system that allows the liquid to flow into the vegetable garden in the backyard, providing it with essential nutrition. Periodically, a fresh layer of dry leaves is added over the old layer. After several layers and intervals, the entire flooring of dry leaves mixed with cow dung and urine is cleared and heaped in a designated area for the manure to ferment, to be used in the paddy fields as needed. Hmm, these scenarios, sounds, and scents are imprinted in my memory for a lifetime.

He mentioned that he worked in Saudi Arabia as a manager at a service station. Working in Saudi Arabia was a significant opportunity for a lower middle-class bloke, as he would earn much more than he would if he did the same work in India. That was the allure of going to these oil-rich Middle Eastern countries. The range of skill sets required was also very broad, from essential to highly sophisticated.

He suggested that I should stop working after marriage. He believed my salary of ₹[12]7,000 was too meagre, and he would support me financially by sending money every month from Saudi Arabia.

"The thought of quitting my job never occurred until he mentioned it. That was never on the cards because no amount of money seemed sufficient for my family. My mind was in turmoil. Should I quit my job after marriage? Would this man truly take care of my family's financial needs? One part of me urged, 'Quit and take life easy.' The

---

12. ₹: Rupee, an Indian rupee, is the official currency of the Republic of India.

daily routine of running around felt too exhausting. On the other hand, given the commitments at home, I wasn't bold enough to give up my job. Any money coming in would be helpful. "Quitting my job was not an option." He also went on to ask if I was seeing anyone; if so, he needed to know immediately to avoid future complications. I assured him I was not. He wanted to ensure that the marriage was not forced upon me.

I remained silent for most of the conversation. I had come here at my Amma's insistence. Now, this man was charming me. Should I reject him or go ahead and marry him? My mind was brimming with questions and confusion.

"Can I have your mobile number?"

The voice jolted me out of my trance. I replied that I didn't use it much. Reluctantly, I gave him my number. It is customary for both parties to return to their respective households, discuss the pros and cons with all family members, and then arrive at a decision.

Sukesh surprised us by telling my brother-in-law on the spot that he liked me. My brother-in-law nodded and said, "We shall get back to you once we discuss it with her mother."

From there, we proceeded to my brother-in-law's nearby house. Another typical agricultural house of coastal Karnataka, similar to Sukesh's but slightly more open, airy, and closer to the coast. By the time I arrived, I had already received a text message from him.

'Hi,' it read. I didn't reply. Then came another message, followed by yet another. Now, I felt obliged to respond.

"I'm at my sister's house," I texted back.

My phone began to ring. I had a basic numeric mobile phone as I could not afford a smartphone. Though the number was unfamiliar, I knew it was him. This wasn't very pleasant. Why had he started calling me so soon? Did he have something personal to discuss or ask before we made a decision? Or was he trying to sway my choice to say yes to him? I found a corner of the house to avoid everyone.

I answered the call. "Hi, it's me, Sukesh," he said.

"I'm sorry, I'm at my sister's house. I'll call you as soon as I get back home."

"Okay, please. I'll wait for your call." This guy seemed to be in a hurry. My elder sister checked on me and asked if I had given my number to him. I said yes.

She disapproved and advised, "You'd better hold it until the family endorses it."

"What should I do if he keeps calling me?" I said in a frustrated tone, much to my sister's discontent. I understood she was being protective of me, but my mind was in such turmoil. My sister, brother-in-law, and I travelled in my brother-in-law's car back home. Throughout the journey, I remained silent, gazing out the window while enjoying the breeze. It was lovely to be in a car, I thought. I was so accustomed to travelling by bus in the searing heat, often sweating and sticking to one another in the overcrowded vehicle. A car, on the other hand, offered privacy. My sister was in the front passenger seat, frequently checking on me.

Upon arriving home, Amma beamed with joy, delighted by her son-in-law's arrival. A son-in-law was always special and received a warm, distinguished welcome. Meanwhile, I headed straight inside to change into something more comfortable, as the saree felt unsuitable for the sweltering heat. As usual, I plunged into the household chores, but I was unusually silent; typically,

I was the chatterbox of the house. I began sweeping the front veranda while my sister seemed hesitant to come and speak to me, wary of my temper.

I could faintly overhear my brother-in-law, Amma, and sister conversing, their voices blending with the sound of the broom in my hand scraping against the floor. It was evident what they were discussing. After tea, my sister and brother-in-law took their leave.

Dinner time is generally early in the villages. After dinner, I was resting at the edge of the sit-out when Amma slowly approached me and sat beside me. I didn't look at her face.

In her usual soothing voice, she asked me with a mischievous smile, "Your groom is handsome, says your sister."

I merely turned my head towards her and met her gaze. I wasn't smiling, nor was I grim. As I looked into her eyes, I saw the silent despair of a widow with two more daughters to marry off.

She continued with a composed voice, "In our situation, we must consider it from all angles. The man is good-looking. The family seems respectable, too. They say he is mild-mannered, works abroad, earns well, and has agreed to marry without a dowry[13]…"

Amma went on and on. I sensed that they had already decided on my behalf. They hadn't even bothered to ask for my opinion.

"Are you alright with this marriage proposal? What do you think?" I regretted having judged my Amma so hastily.

In a low, unassuming voice and with no visible emotion on my face, looking away from her expectant gaze, I replied, "I don't know, Amma. It looks fine. If all of you are okay with it, I'm okay with it, too." That was the standard response of an Indian girl in those days! I didn't have the heart to argue with the poor lady.

There had been no formal reply from our family yet. My mother had asked for a week to decide. By this time, I was working as a lab assistant at St. Thomas Medical College, Mangalore. I travelled from Udupi by the college bus. Although he texted me frequently, I replied very selectively. Somehow, I was instinctively aware of my limits. Conservative family, conservative

---

13. Dowry: Money given by the bride's family to the groom during marriage.

village folk. I wanted to maintain my distance until the marriage and avoid giving any room for gossip. One day, while on the bus returning from Mangalore, I noticed a car following us. It would overtake us and then fall back, repeating this in several loops. To my utter disbelief, I realised it was him! For some reason, I felt quite frightened, and my heart sank.

My phone rang. It was him. I answered the call. "Hi…" he said from the other end.

"….." I was taken aback.

"Just following your bus…" I could sense his grin when he said that.

"But why?"

"Just like that." I didn't know what to say, so I just ended the call. I felt genuinely scared; I wasn't used to this. I had never romanced anyone or had a crush on anyone before. I never had the time for it, nor had anyone tried to woo me. This was all new. Moreover, my family had not yet replied to them. If not for the sound of the bus engine and the gushing wind through the windows, I was certain my heartbeat could be heard by the person sitting next to me.

My bus was scheduled to arrive in Udupi at 6:30 pm. When I disembarked, I feared that Sukesh would be waiting for me. My heart began to race uncontrollably. As the bus reached my destination, there he was, holding a single long-stemmed rose.

"Hi…." He spoke with a mischievous glint in his eyes, effortlessly playing the role of a seasoned romantic.

"Hi…." I replied, blushing from head to toe. What was happening to me? I had never experienced this before. After an awkward silence, he handed me the rose.

"Thanks…." I think my heartbeat was louder than my voice.

"Come, I'll drop you home in the car."

"No… please. I'll manage," I said, blushing again. I could barely stand straight, my body twisting at awkward angles as if every joint refused to cooperate.

"It's alright; I can drop you at your house. We can chat on the way and get to know each other better." His friend was with him, too; he was the one who had accompanied him to the temple the other day.

"You know it's risky. If anyone from my village sees me stepping out of a car with strangers, tongues will start wagging."

"So what? We are getting married anyway."

"But we aren't yet." My voice returned to normal. I was surprised by the sternness in my reply.

"C'mon, please. I insist." I didn't have the heart to say no. Perhaps I enjoyed this newfound attention as well. Nobody had ever given me this kind of attention before. I felt both nervous and happy at the same time.

"Alright, please drop me at the bus stop near the riverbank."

"Fine," he said with a gleam of satisfaction, his persistence having paid off. I hopped into the back seat of the small car. It was growing dark. He asked me random questions, and I answered them.

Suddenly, he told his friend, "Switch on the dome light; I need to see my girl clearly." My face burned with embarrassment. I didn't know how to respond. Finally, my stop arrived. "You travel this far daily? Oh dear!" There was genuine concern in his voice. All I knew was the struggle in life. I was unaccustomed to such soothing words and this display of concern. "My girl...," echoed in my head.

I walked toward the boat, waving goodbye to him, my steps still unsteady. I could feel his gaze on me from behind, making me even more self-conscious. The awkwardness was almost overwhelming, and I had a strong urge to turn back and look at him. Perhaps it was an instinct for a girl? I had seen this very moment immortalized in movies—most memorably by Kajol and Shah Rukh Khan in *Dilwale Dulhania Le Jayenge.*

Were you wondering why I was walking towards the boat? As I mentioned at the beginning, my village was frozen in time. The boat was the lifeline of our village, as crossing the river was the shortest route to the nearby town or bus stop, from where we could connect to other towns. We had to arrive on time when the boat set off from the riverbank to take us further on our journey to school, college, or work. Otherwise, we would have to take a long, roundabout walk to the nearest bus stop.

During the monsoon season, we faced a different set of challenges. The river water would swell to dangerously high levels. The boatman would forewarn us that there would be no crossings on such days. However, some of us students had exams, and there was no way we could skip them. The boatman, however, could not grasp the significance of the exam. He would chide us, saying, "Are your exams more important than your lives?" Though he had a valid point, we begged, pleaded, and cried to be taken across the river. Now, when I look back, standing on the banks of the 500-foot-wide river, I wonder why on earth we crossed the river at such dangerous water levels. What a risk that was.

There was a set timetable for the boat service. The last boat crossing was at 6:30 in the evening. Therefore, we had to be there by that time at any cost. That was why I had never experienced city life after sunset in Mangalore, Manipal or Udupi, which I crossed daily. Due to the fear of missing the boat, I had never attended any cultural day at college, as these always commenced after sunset. I used to feel embarrassed to tell my lecturers and friends why I wouldn't stay for the cultural day at college. I couldn't disclose that I travelled home by boat; it sounded too primitive.

The signal to call the boatman from the other side of the riverbank was a loud "Koo." We would "Koo" from quite a distance from the river to let the boatman know we were on our way and that he should wait for us. If we reached the riverbank after the boat had set off, we would be scolded for not "Koo-ing" in advance.

The cost of crossing the river both ways was ₹1. We had to pay him around ₹30 once a month. During my college days, I would dread the end of the month as the boatman would ask for money from all the students, and I wouldn't have it. I was spared this humiliation in front of others since the boatman never asked me, allowing me to pay him once every two or three months. He was very kind and understanding, possibly because he knew my household lacked male earning members.

I was so nervous. I prayed that no one had seen me leaving a stranger's car. Once I reached home, I did not dare to tell Amma. I wasn't sure how she would react. My younger sister was my only confidante. I was writhing like a fish out of water. I had to confide in someone. She watched me for a while, then approached me and asked, "What's up with you? You seem so lost.

Is everything alright?" So much for being a sister. Being born from the same womb creates a connection that allows us to assess each other intuitively. I confided in her about what had happened. She gave me a cheeky smile.

I said, "Shut up…." pretending to be angry.

The following day, I heard the SMS notification beep. I knew it was him. I reached for my mobile and slowly opened the SMS. There it was.

'I love you!'

I didn't know how to respond! Nobody had ever said that to me before. And how does that happen? We've hardly known each other. What does "falling in love" mean between people? Isn't it more physical than emotional? At least, in this case, I thought so. Love is sacrosanct, in my opinion. It comes with a great deal of emotional attachment to anything or anyone. You do not simply fall in love with someone. You may feel an attraction for someone instantly. But that isn't love. I don't comprehend the notion of 'Love at first sight'. That's infatuation; that's lust. It cannot be love. Love must be nurtured over time, like good wine. They say some of the most expensive wines in the world are aged in casks for years to develop the right flavours and taste. That's how love should be. You meet someone, feel attracted to them, get to know them, start to appreciate some of their traits, dislike a few, admire how they treat you, and find common interests. The relationship fosters the strength to confide in one another. You enjoy each other's company; you like spending time together. You get an automatic smile on your face when you see them, regardless of how difficult your day may have been. You begin to miss them if you don't see them for a while, and only then perhaps you realise there is something special between you two. I believe that should be falling in love.

And here he was saying he loved me when he hardly knew me. But isn't that the case with most marriages in this country? Two strangers get married and fall in love later, or perhaps not. Yet, I've seen my parents so deeply in love with each other. I have never seen them argue. They could sit for hours on the veranda, talking. I've watched my Pappa stick flowers in Amma's hair and admire her in a saree with dreamy eyes and a transfixed smile on his face. It is possible to fall in love after marriage too, isn't it? I'm not certain. Let's see.

Then he texted, "Why don't you reply? Don't you like me?"

I still took my time. I had to complete all my morning chores. I replied on my way to Mangalore after settling onto the bus. I had to think it over for a while before I responded to him. I was not in a rush.

I took a deep breath and texted back, "It's not about whether I like you or not. If I say yes now, the marriage preparations will commence. My family is not financially in a position to arrange my marriage. I need time to gather finances."

He replied, "I shall not burden your family. I'm sure we could work out the financial details between us. I'll assist you with it. However, I'm not in a position to wait that long. I need to return to Saudi Arabia shortly. Before that, we need to get at least engaged. It would be helpful if your family could respond positively soon. And if you do not wish to proceed with this alliance, that too is acceptable to me." I could sense the urgency in his words, yet I also appreciated his gentlemanly attitude. I did a lot of thinking for the next three to four days. I swayed between "Yes" and "No". There were too many variables.

But then, in the best interest of everyone, I weighed in and said, "Yes." I could sense the joy in his voice once again. I could perceive his emotions through our phone calls now. I suppose that was a good sign for a relationship—when you can judge the other person's mood without actually seeing them.

After I said 'yes,' his calls became more frequent. He seemed genuinely thoughtful and caring, promising to look after my family and even support my sister's education. That touched me deeply—I had never experienced such sincere concern from someone outside my own family. His outpouring of love and care left me in awe, so much so that I had no questions for him; he effortlessly won us over. Every weekend, he took me, my sister, and my aunt's daughter out, and we thoroughly enjoyed his company.

He informed me that he had a business in Saudi Arabia. What was his business? How much did he earn? Where will I be after marriage? How will we manage the household? How will we sort out the expenses? How will our life be post-marriage? I wonder why I didn't have all these questions. I had no counter questions. It was a one-way street. The very fact that someone was ready to marry me was, in itself, a significant thing. In those days, "No Dowry", "Foreign Job", and "No Jewellery Demand" were the best things that could happen to a girl's family. Given our financial situation, these were my most compelling reasons to say yes. All the other questions were pushed aside. For me, no further details were necessary. He worked abroad, so it was assumed he should be earning well. That was all that mattered. He had also assured me that he would take me to Saudi Arabia as soon as possible post-marriage. I appreciated the way he treated my Amma and my sister. Yes, it was an overwhelming experience. It felt like a dream.

Now, back to my story. Where was I? It's been just three days since I got married, and I was at my in-laws' house.

A New Home, A Hidden Truth

It was the fourth day after our wedding. This was the beginning of my 'labour term'. From that day onwards, every other household work was piled on me. It began in the morning with kitchen work, cow shed upkeep, mopping the entire house, washing the clothes, washing the utensils, cooking three times a day and not to mention the innumerable times I had to prepare tea, bring water into the house from the well (There was no overhead water tank), fill the large drum with water in the bathroom and heat it with firewood. There was no mixer or grinder; we had to grind the masala [14] for the food using a large stone grinder by hand. Though my mother-in-law used to pitch in, I was totally preoccupied from the time I woke up till I hit the bed at night. And then, at night, I had to be available for my husband, as, after all, we were newly married. I was dead tired. This did not make any sense. I could not take it physically and it was breaking me mentally. I wondered who did all this before my arrival. The three sisters of my husband seemed to be testing my will. Every day, I was on the verge of crying as the night arrived.

---

14. Masala: A mixture of ground spices used in Indian cooking

Growing up in an agricultural family, hard manual labour was nothing new to me. But the work was shared among all the family members. But here, it was all loaded on me. Nobody was sharing the work except my aged mother-in-law. I felt exploited. I was furious and frustrated. How could they treat a newlywed girl like this? Have they got a wife for their brother or a maid? I was about to explode. Unfortunately, this was not my house where I could vent my anger. Within a week, I mustered the courage to tell my husband this was getting too much for me. My legs, back, and head were aching. Sukesh asked me to endure it until the wedding guests had departed. He assured me that we would be alone with his parents and that things would improve. It's the time of desperation that one remembers their home. I was already longing to go home and see my Amma and yearning for that hug, for that love, for that special taste of food made by her.

My Amma grew up in dire poverty in a farming household. Although they had enough food from growing rice and vegetables at home, no money was available for anything else. She was stunning in her younger days, as vouched for by our neighbours and relatives. She was just 45 when my father passed away. Her entire life followed a strict routine from morning until night, with no deviation whatsoever. God knows what would have been running in her mind at various stages of her struggle. But she never showed it on her face or in her behaviour. She had unwavering faith in her three daughters. Yes, three daughters. One was older than me, and one was younger. She was always encouraging and granted us complete freedom. She exhibited mental resilience, coupled with a strong sense of self-respect and pride. She would not beg for money from anyone. Somehow, she would accumulate barely enough money to scrape through.

There were certain things that we could not understand at that age. Once in a while, she opens up these days and tells stories of her past struggles. For instance, the local village grocer would see her from afar and know she needed some groceries on credit. He used to make her wait till the other customers were attended to and finally, with reluctance, acknowledged her presence. This was embarrassing for my mother, but she had little or no choice.

My mother was a typical, simple village girl whose ultimate dream was to have a good, strong house. She used to go and check on other homes in the village that were being rebuilt. She would come back and describe all that in great detail and with such excitement without a tinge of jealousy. It sounded as though her own house was being built. Such a simpleton she was.

Just as a new routine was settling in, I was shocked to see Sukesh in a different light one evening. I was shaken at the sight of him. The man was drunk. I had never witnessed a drunken man so closely before. He was unable to stand upright and was all over the place. His head hung down; he could not lift it. His family members admonished him for not changing his behaviour even after getting married. Did they just say, "Even after getting married?"

I froze! I couldn't comprehend what was happening. How could he be drinking like this? He had no control over himself. He slumped in one of the corner chairs in the living room, sulking and looking as if he would topple off. His father was yelling incessantly at one end. I stood in our bedroom doorway, watching in disbelief as the drama unfolded in the living area. His mother slowly emerged from the kitchen with a plate of food. He was certainly not in a position to eat. To my astonishment, his elderly mother began feeding this grown man! Oh God! I had never witnessed anything like this. I felt lightheaded. Was the earth spinning, or was it merely my mind?

My dream flight crash-landed. Nobody had informed me of this side of Sukesh. Yes… the side effects of an arranged marriage. Yet, the second most populous country in the world marries this way. Where did this population arise from if arranged marriages didn't work? This was kept from me. This was his family's secret: *his alcohol addiction*. He was led to the bedroom by his sisters. He was not in a position to change his clothes. I looked at the almost lifeless body of my husband on the bed. I stared briefly and then slept on the floor on a mat and pillow. The smell emanating from his open mouth was repulsive.

The following morning, I confronted him, "What the hell was that?"

The charmer that he was said, "Hey, no. I don't usually drink this much. I was feeling a bit stressed. That's why I went a little overboard. Otherwise, I don't drink much. I swear."

I wasn't sure whether to believe him. Part of me wished his words were true, while another part was still in shock. Over the next few nights, I noticed he would wake in the middle of the night and sneak out. Growing up in a village, we were used to waking at even the slightest sound. Initially, I assumed he was going out to relieve himself. One night, I awoke and quietly followed him. To my astonishment, he was having a drink in the kitchen. Now, I was certain he was struggling with alcohol addiction.

I ended up in a tricky situation, not knowing what to do. What should I do? My mind began to race in circles. Where will this lead? Will it be like this for the rest of my married life? Will he start hitting me as they do in the movies? What if he actually starts hitting me? How should I react? Will this marriage last? Should I stay in this marriage or end it? Should I try to convince him? Can I reform his ways? But then I reminded myself that this marriage was arranged by my family with great difficulty. How do I tell my Amma, my sisters, or others? I felt lost. I felt cheated! Why me? I ran out of tears. I couldn't cry, no matter how overwhelmed I was. I just couldn't. I couldn't find that release.

A month passed, and the guests had all departed. The four of us were at home: his parents, him, and me. Wherever we went, he would somehow trick me into letting him get high on a few drinks. I was clueless as to when he would leave and when he would drink. I tried to convince him repeatedly. Whenever I spoke to him about it, he would agree lovingly, saying, "Okay, I will stop from now on. I will stop for your sake." Yet the next day, he would be at it again. He was blatantly lying. He was using me, exploiting my situation and emotions.

I confronted my father-in-law, a man in his late 70s. He was a person of very few words. Frail-looking, tall, and physically strong, he had farmed all his life. He remained very active, going to the farm and the paddy fields every morning after breakfast and returning only in the afternoon for lunch and then a siesta. After his nap, he would have a cup of tea before heading back to the fields. He would return, take a bath, and by evening, go to the nearby town to meet and chat with his friends, coming home only for dinner. This was his daily routine.

He wasn't often available to talk with family members. Whenever I looked at him, I was reminded of my father. Though there were no similarities between them, somehow, he evoked memories of him.

My Pappa was a good-looking, tall man with thick spectacles. Although soft-spoken, he was a strict disciplinarian. He never liked us idling about. He wanted us to be very neatly dressed and our hair properly combed; the way we sat, the way we talked, and the way we behaved were all overseen by our father. He insisted that we iron our uniforms using a coal-heated iron box before sending us to school. It might be considered sexist for me to say he groomed us three girls to be the men of the house; rather, he prepared us to handle all the tasks around the house without any discrimination. He did not hesitate to use the cane occasionally when we misbehaved. However, looking back, I realise it was a normal childhood. I have vivid memories of our primary school days when our birthdays were celebrated, as they were quite uncommon in my village. My father was loving towards us and our mother. He wasn't highly educated and tried his hand at a few businesses, but when success eluded him, he ultimately had to settle down in our village with my Amma and become an agriculturist. He was well-respected and well-loved in our village.

No one in our house would talk back to him. His decision was final and binding. He suffered from chronic asthma, and his lungs were failing. He was admitted to the hospital one day when he could no longer cope, and he passed away at the age of 56 while I was just 18.

His death created a significant void in our family. Suddenly, the house was home to four women and my grandfather, who was counting down his days. We were all in the dark about what was happening. It was an incredibly confusing time for us.

I took on my father-in-law one day. I was trembling with anger but managed to keep my tone respectful. I asked him, "How could you do this to me? Would you have given your daughter in marriage to a drunkard? What right did you have to ruin my life? Doesn't your conscience prick you?" Silence! That's all the answer I got. Absolute silence! But I had to vent it out on someone, so I did on him.

I even threatened Sukesh with a divorce if he continued like this, but it was in vain. Whenever I said so, he would emotionally blackmail me. That he could not live without me and that he would kill himself if I left him, etc., etc. Though I threatened him, I don't think I dared to leave him. Not that I was attached to him, but society would have broken my home. My Amma and my sisters would have to undergo all the torture.

I found myself questioning why he was drinking so much. Four months into our marriage, he was not giving me any indication of returning to Saudi Arabia for his job. I couldn't help but wonder why. When we first met, he seemed eager to go back. Now, after our marriage, why had he remained for four months? Does he not have to return? What on earth was happening?

I decided to ask him one day. Coincidentally, one of his sisters was home that day, and she asked him the same question. I overheard it. He replied that he had incurred heavy losses in his business in Saudi Arabia and was not in a position to go back! One after the other, my life didn't seem to be a smooth ride. I was meant to live like this, I suppose. The discussion continued among him, his sister, her husband, and his father. Nobody discussed it with me. They didn't find it important enough, I suppose.

Looking back, I felt nobody would have offered him a girl to wed. I was the scapegoat. Everyone knew about his drinking problem. They wanted a bride from a poor family to marry him so that no one would question them later. Gradually, he started opening up to me. He would discuss everything with me except his alcoholism. And even after getting drunk, it wasn't as if he would abuse me or get physical. He would shout at his sisters but never at me. Never! He had a soft spot for me. But he was addicted to alcohol.

Finally, around mid-May, five months into our marriage, he left for Saudi Arabia. He mentioned that he would seek some opportunities there. I let out a sigh of relief. At last, things seemed to be on track. After his departure to Saudi Arabia, I lived with my in-laws. Occasionally, I would visit my sister's house in the nearby town, thirty minutes away. I also returned home to see Amma once. Sukesh would call twice a week.

Everything seemed fine when, out of the blue, he appeared at our doorstep on 11th July! I sensed something was amiss. That night, after a couple of drinks, he mentioned that things hadn't gone as planned. He said he would return in another two weeks. The following morning, one of his sisters, Prathibha, who lived in Mumbai, called me. She gave me another shocker.

"Your husband has borrowed money from me for his business in Saudi. Ask him about it and tell me when he will repay me." I wondered why she wasn't asking her brother directly. Why was she routing it through me? She never consulted me when giving him the loan. Why should I be the one asking him? I didn't want to get involved in their affairs. I kept to myself.

After a few days, she called again, "We plan to buy a flat in Mumbai. We are short of money. Why don't you sell your gold and repay me? Anyway, your husband owes us."

I didn't want to confront her straightaway. I said, "*Akka*[15], I am not aware of any transactions between you siblings. You should speak to him directly and sort it out. I am not currently employed; otherwise, I might have been able to offer you some financial assistance." I thought this would ward her off.

---

15. Akka: Elder sister

However, she began pestering me daily after that. "Please do this favour for us. If not for him, we would have had this house by now. At least, give it to me as a loan. I'll pay you back after three months once I am able to draw money from the *Chit fund* [16] that I have been investing."

I found myself in a dilemma. Should I give her the money, or should I refrain? Would she cause trouble for my husband, leading him to drink more? Should I confide in Sukesh about this? What if he argued with his sister? I contemplated selling the four bangles my in-laws had given me at my wedding. However, I could not bear to part with something my Amma had bestowed upon me. The Gold chain. There was no way I would sell that off.

Both my in-laws were good to me. I gathered the courage to ask my Father-in-law what to do. He said, "It's okay. You give it to them, and let's see. I'll get it back to you after some time."

---

16. Chit fund: A chit fund is a financial arrangement where a group of individuals pool money regularly, and one member receives the pooled sum each cycle, typically through bidding or a lottery system

I found myself in quite a predicament. I asked Sukesh what I should do. He, too, suggested that I go ahead and pawn it. We could retrieve it later. With a green light all around, I pawned the four bangles given by my in-laws and also the chain given by my Amma. His sister expressed her gratitude for the gesture and promised to return it within three months.

It somehow never came back to me. I asked them for it many times but only received insults in return. Eventually, I realised that they had gifted me those bangles intending to take them back after some time. That was their master plan, and each one was complicit in this. One day, Sukesh asked his father if he could sell part of the property, as he needed money to return to Saudi Arabia because he was in deep trouble. My father-in-law flatly refused.

Sukesh claimed that he, too, had contributed financially many times to the development of the farm over the years. He told me that at the age of eight, he went to Mumbai to work in hotels as a daily wage labourer. Gradually rising from obscurity, he had married off two of his three sisters. He assisted in rebuilding the current house. He went to Saudi Arabia to work for the family's welfare. He also supported his eldest sister when her husband faced severe financial difficulties. He asserted he had endured a very tough life. Yet today, his father refused to sell a small portion of land when he was distressed. This made him feel quite bad. However, I thought my father-in-law was right in his way. They would be left with nothing if he kept selling his land to meet Sukesh's needs. On the other hand, I pondered the point of having all that land if it could not be used when the family required it.

I contemplated whether I would treat my sisters similarly if they were in need. The bond between us was filled with such love.

Shalini was quite naïve by nature. Elder to me by three years, she was good-looking, fair-complexioned, with a round face, dark eyes, long hair, a graceful figure, and a natural elegance in how she carried herself. She was not particularly inclined towards academics and, after 10th grade, wished to discontinue her studies. The situation at home was such that she was compelled to find a job. A temporary teacher vacancy at our village's government-run school arose. She was offered ₹600 per month for this position. She readily accepted. Imagine! ₹600 per month! On her salary day, she would excitedly pick up groceries. Given the financial situation, every single penny was accounted for.

Without warning, she lost her job one day as a permanent teacher was appointed at the school. Now, she was compelled to find a job as a tailor in a garment factory in the nearby town of Manipal, which was 10 kilometres away. There, the supervisor noticed her as he was looking for a bride for his younger brother. My sister was just 19 then. She was very good-looking, so the groom agreed to marry her without dowry. He said he wouldn't force it on her, but it was up to her to agree. My sister lacked the maturity to decide her marriage. She agreed to whatever our parents had to say about the alliance. My Amma was very keen to go ahead with this alliance as she had two more girls to be married off.

My Pappa also approved of the proposal. The groom was employed at a hotel in Mumbai. My Pappa travelled to Mumbai to discuss matters with him. In our family, the men decided whom their daughters or sisters would marry. Rarely was the girl's opinion sought in those days. However, after meeting the prospective groom, my Pappa had a progressive mindset for those times, asking my sister if she wished to proceed with the proposal. "Dowry" was a common practice then, and we did not have the financial means to offer one. The boy had agreed to marry without any demands for 'dowry' and was doing reasonably well in life. The inclination to say 'Yes' was quite strong from all sides. Yet, my father showed great consideration by asking her opinion. Whether he would have agreed if she had said 'No' remains a matter of speculation.

Even without "Dowry", the marriage was an expensive affair, but we managed to conduct it with some degree of difficulty.

We were quite happy to have a brother-in-law in the family. Though he was somewhat reserved, he took good care of my sister. Not that we were particularly close. Perhaps he didn't want to bond with us too much, as we were two more girls to marry off, which would mean a significant financial responsibility for him. That was no fault of his, however. He was, on the whole, a fairly good person. There was no doubt about that.

A Voyage into Uncertainty

Another two months passed. This was September. I could sense Sukesh's frustration and I was all the more frustrated. It didn't look like he was returning to Saudi, and money was also running out.

One day, Sukesh told me, "I'm fed up with my ungrateful family. I want to leave home and go away. I don't want anything to do with these people anymore."

I said, "Where do you plan to go? Just like that, we pack and go? Where to? Where do we live? How do we manage without money?"

I was apprehensive about taking his side due to his drinking habits. I was uncertain about him and couldn't share this with my Amma for fear of worrying her. I wanted to confide in someone, so I spoke with my aunt, Amma's younger sister. She lived in a town called Davangere, about a five-hour drive from here. She listened patiently to my entire story and was taken aback. It took her some time to regain her composure. None of the family knew what I was enduring in my married life till now.

She said, "Where can you two go like that? If you are that desperate and have decided, why don't you come to our house in Davangere?" My aunt's situation was no different from ours. Her husband worked as a waiter in a restaurant, and she contributed to the household finances by tailoring clothes at home. They had a daughter in the fifth standard. I knew their income was modest, barely sufficient for their needs. Nevertheless, she was like my mother and generously offered us shelter. I didn't want to impose on her, but Sukesh behaved erratically. He was determined to leave the house. No amount of reasoning seemed to penetrate his mind.

I told her, "Let me see, Aunty, if I can persuade him to change his mind. If he still decides to leave the house, I have no choice but to accompany him. How can I remain at my in-laws' without him? I also can't tell Amma; she would be heartbroken. I haven't shared anything with anyone except you. Thank you so much for being there for me. I'll let you know if we choose to come over. But coming over to do what? I don't want to burden you any further, Aunty."

"You are no different than my daughter. You may find some job here. Both of you. This is a nice town. We can somehow make a living here. Don't worry. Let me know."

"Okay…" I wasn't sure if she meant what she said. Not that I blamed her, but I knew she herself was in a very difficult financial situation.

I discussed my conversation with Sukesh. He listened quietly. During the night, he said, "Let's leave tomorrow after Pappa and Amma have gone out to the fields." I asked, "Why? Why must we leave without telling them? Let's not do that. It's not right. Let's tell them we are going to my aunt's place for a short time. There's nothing wrong with that."

"No! When they can be so obstinate that they can't assist me in my hour of need, there is no way I want to share anything happening in my life. Let's go." He was not in the mood for reasoning. I was in a complete fix.

The next morning, after my in-laws began their routine farm work, we packed two bags and left home for Davangere without informing anyone. I called my aunt as soon as we boarded the bus. Nobody knew where we were—not Sukesh's family nor mine. I felt guilt-ridden. Everything was happening so quickly that I didn't even have time to think. We arrived in Davangere around 6 pm. My aunt's husband came to the bus station to meet us. We hopped into an auto-rickshaw and went straight to their house. It was a small one-room kitchen house, just right for two people, but they also had their six-year-old daughter. Our presence in the already cramped space was suffocating. My aunt welcomed us with a big, warm smile. We spent some time chatting before retiring for the night.

Meanwhile, my conscience was pricking at me. The next day, I mustered all my courage to call Amma. I still didn't tell her we were with my aunt in Davangere. With a heavy heart, I lied to her and said we had left for Bangalore. Never, as far as I can remember, had I ever lied to her. The feeling was quite cringeworthy. Guilt was overtaking me from head to toe. I could feel my heart palpitating. I wasn't sure I had convinced her of my situation, that I had to accompany Sukesh without much choice. With the calmness in her voice still intact, she said, "I know you are in Davangere, not Bangalore. Tell me the truth. (Pause) Where would you go in Bangalore?" Being my Amma, she could sense it, or perhaps my aunt had mentioned it without my knowledge.

The dam that had been holding back all my emotions burst open. I broke down. I couldn't control it any longer. Amma was one dear person with whom I had to confide everything in my life. However, since my marriage, I hadn't told her anything for fear of hurting her. I kept sobbing and recounting everything that had been happening. I had no better choice but to release my pent-up emotions. Meanwhile, Amma was a silent listener on the other end. I knew she was a rock-solid, strong lady, but I didn't realise she was this strong. She said, "If you believe this marriage isn't working, then come over. We can still manage two meals a day. Don't lead a miserable life. But remember, I won't be there for you forever. Sooner or later, I shall have to go, and don't regret your decision at that time." That was a very strong and bold statement to be made by someone born and raised in a rural setting where separation and divorce are unheard of.

Amma also mentioned that my sisters-in-law had phoned her the same day we went missing and began to abuse her, to her utter dismay and shock. Amma had no idea what was happening since she was unaware of our plans. She said they were taking all sorts of liberties in abusing her. They went so far as to tell her that I had kidnapped Sukesh and that if we didn't return within 24 hours, they would file a police complaint regarding some theft. I could feel the tightness in my chest. The guilt of having made my mother endure this was burning me within.

There was a long pause. Both of us held the phone in silence. Our hearts were intertwined, much like a mother's umbilical cord to her child. I drew my solace and strength from that connection through the phone. I finally said

"Bye Amma"

The following day, my aunt's husband secured a job for Sukesh as a restaurant manager. I felt relieved for once. I didn't want to be a burden on my aunt's family. I wanted to move out of my aunt's house as soon as possible. I also needed to find a job. Otherwise, I knew we wouldn't be able to make ends meet.

After a month, we borrowed some money from my aunt and found a house to rent nearby. I felt relieved. I borrowed a few essential utensils from my aunt and purchased a few more. In the meantime, I was searching for a job as a lab technician.

I had completed the three-year Diploma in Medical Lab Technology soon after my 12th and began working as a lab technician in Udupi town for a salary of ₹2,000 per month.

This was insufficient to support myself, my amma and my younger sister, as I had an education loan to repay, my younger sister's college fees and other incidentals to care for. In the meantime, a job vacancy arose in the nearby town of Kundapura, 60 km from Udupi, where I currently work. The salary offered was double what I was earning, and the owner allowed me and another lady staff member to stay in their house. This was a blessing, as the increased pay enabled me to settle my commitments, cover my younger sister's college fees, and still send some money to Amma. We had also taken out additional loans for my elder sister's marriage, making my EMIs quite high.

After some time in Kundapura, I received a better offer from St. Thomas Medical College in Mangalore, where the salary was ₹ 7,000. I eagerly accepted the offer. However, I didn't have the luxury of living in Mangalore, a larger city and district headquarters, with a much higher cost of living. I needed to travel 70 km one way from my village. The road link to our village was roundabout and lengthy on foot. The nearest access to the bus stop required crossing the river. I had to wake up at 4:30 am, prepare my meal, pack my lunch, get ready, and catch the first boat across the river, the only way to reach the nearest bus stop. I needed to walk 3 km from the opposite bank to the closest point where I could catch a bus bound for Udupi. From Udupi, the college bus would then transport us to Mangalore. If I missed the college bus, I had to take a private bus to Mangalore city, which imposed an additional expense I could hardly afford. The same routine was reversed in the evening, and by the time I reached home, it would be around 7:30 pm.

It was a Sunday, and it had been just over a month and a half since we moved to Davangere. One of Sukesh's friends from Saudi Arabia called him. He excitedly answered the call and walked out of the house. He returned after 20 minutes, his face gleaming.

"My friend Hasan called. He is asking me to come over to Saudi. He says there is a business opportunity there."

"What kind of business?" I was not willing to take it at face value this time.

"I told you earlier, right? Brokering visa issuance to labourers. It's a bit risky but highly profitable. Hasan is willing to invest money. Not much is required. Within 6 months to a year, we could earn very well. I'll take you with me in 6 months, away from all this nonsense. Let's build a new life there. You could visit India once or twice a year to see your Amma. I don't want to come back anymore. I've given enough money to my family all these years without keeping anything for myself. A mistake that I made. Today, they are unwilling to help me out. It's time I thought about myself and my family. I need to be selfish too." He was so excited and happy. It had been a long time since I had seen him like this. I thought to myself that all this was going to end well. I did not respond to him at all. I was happy, but I was wary, too. He had not been drinking ever since we came to Davangere. I observed that he did not drink when he was busy.

One more month passed, and then one day, towards the end of November, he received his visa. His friend had also sent him a flight ticket. I hadn't menstruated, which led me to doubt whether I had conceived. I purchased a testing kit. To our excitement, the test was positive. Everyone around was thrilled. Sukesh was on cloud nine. "I need a daughter, please," was his first reaction!

I called Amma to share the news. She was excited as well. I assumed my life was finally returning to normal. The possibility of me getting pregnant seemed to be a good omen.

The day of Sukesh's travel arrived. My aunt and I decided to accompany him to Bangalore International Airport. Wow, I had never been to an airport in my life. It was so huge. It looked like a large mall. I wished him luck and waved goodbye. I had tears in my eyes. It was more out of joy. I thought God had answered my prayers. Things should be fine from now on. My aunt and I loitered around for some time. We were hungry and wanted to eat. We spent some time around various restaurants outside the airport. There was nowhere that we could eat as they were so prohibitively expensive. Do people eat here? Oh yes, they do. All the restaurants were surprisingly jam-packed! Wow, what kind of money do people have? And look where we were! We couldn't afford even one item on their menu. We took the airport bus straight to the intercity bus stand. We had a good meal at one of the restaurants at the bus stand and returned to Davangere.

Meanwhile, back home, an unpleasant situation was unfolding. His sisters were calling Amma and verbally abusing her almost every other day. They were extremely rude to her. I considered calling them and ending this once and for all. However, Sukesh had asked me not to. He had promised to speak to them once he reached Saudi Arabia and resolve the matter. He used to call me once a week. He said everything was fine and would start sending me money soon. He had given me some money before leaving, which would last me for another two weeks. My aunt pressured me to move back in with her and not waste money on rent. I asked Sukesh, and he agreed. I moved back to my aunt's house, but I couldn't shake the feeling that I was intruding on their privacy. There was no separate bedroom; it was merely a hall where we all slept. My niece grew fond of me, and I would take care of her when she returned from half-day school.

The houses in cities were remarkably small and compact. The air was polluted, water was scarce, and the places were overcrowded. I didn't particularly enjoy life here. My village, in contrast, was pristine and clean, with ample space, greenery, and fresh air. Given the choice, my village environment was worth living in for a lifetime.

A month had passed since Sukesh left, and he still hadn't sent me any money. When I inquired, he promised that he would send it the following week. However, when the next week came, there was nothing. I needed to attend my routine check-ups due to severe nausea from my advancing pregnancy, yet I had no money left. I couldn't ask my aunt for help, so I had to skip my regular appointments. Noticing this, my aunt began to monitor my check-up schedule and insisted on taking me to the doctor.

Sukesh's sisters had ceased calling Amma, who had developed a thick skin to their abuse. During my regular phone call with Sukesh in the second week of January, he said he was coming back the following Wednesday, without providing any reason! I was so naïve that I didn't even inquire why he was returning. I thought it was merely part of his usual travel plans. I was excited to see him and to share my baby bump with him.

"I don't have a direct flight. I'll come via Dubai to Bangalore. I'll head directly to Davangere from there," he said. Pregnancy is a completely different experience. Deep down, I wanted Sukesh to be beside me to share in the joy of pregnancy together. There were three girls in my family. My aunt and my elder sister each had a daughter. We had a significant number of girls in our family, and now Sukesh wanted a girl child as well. For some strange reason, I felt neutral about it. Perhaps because it was my first child? The gender didn't matter to me. I just wanted a healthy baby.

Gone With the Wind

On Wednesday, Sukesh called me from Dubai. "Hi, honey, I just landed in Dubai from Saudi Arabia. I have got a flight to catch to Bangalore in another...." The call dropped!

I waited for his call again. Nothing. It was almost five minutes. He didn't call. Sukesh used to call me from a public booth through a calling card, as it was cheaper. Hence, I couldn't call him back. I tried several times to call his regular number but in vain. I dropped him WhatsApp messages and messages on Facebook Messenger, now that I had a smartphone that Sukesh had bought for me just before our marriage. Nothing!

I couldn't reach him, and I was worried. Why wasn't his phone reachable? If the battery was discharged, he would have charged it by now. He wouldn't have kept the call incomplete. A day passed, and still, there was no sign of his phone call. He should have reached Bangalore by now and been in Davangere according to the schedule.

My aunt was also worried by this point. I felt like calling Amma, my emotional anchor. I yearned to hug her and find that reassuring solace. The power of a mother's hug must be the most potent antidote to all the problems in the world. There is a certain magic in that touch. It makes you feel a part of her. You can sense the transfer of healing energy flowing into your body and mind. I told my aunt, "Let's go home to Bejjolli." She agreed, and we boarded the night sleeper bus—my aunt, her daughter, and I.

We reached home in the morning, and the first thing I did was hug Amma and cry. The magic of her soothing words worked, and we sat down to have breakfast after freshening up. I tried to call Sukesh continuously for the next three to four days but could not reach him. His phone was completely unreachable. I wondered what to do. Should we file a police complaint? What would I say to the police? That my husband has gone missing in Dubai? All sorts of scenarios began running through my mind. Is he hurt? Did someone rob him? No, that can't be; I've heard there's no crime in Dubai. What else could it be? Did he have a heart attack or any health issues? Is he in the hospital? How will I know? There was a train of thoughts going around in circles in my mind.

I was left clueless about what to do. None of us knew what to do. I wanted to see if he had called my in-laws.

Did they have any idea what had happened? Where was he? I was not in touch with my sisters-in-law after our running away incident; I wasn't speaking to them. But now I had no other option but to talk to them.

I mustered some courage and called his second sister in Mumbai. She began shouting at me and blaming me for all the mishaps. I had to endure her expletives. I had to beg her to forgive me and ask for help searching for my husband. Finally, she relented and said, "Alright, give us some time to think, and we will let you know the next course of action—whether to file a missing person complaint or not."

I started calling Sukesh's sister daily, asking her what to do. She seemed to be brushing me off. After about a week, she stopped responding altogether. I didn't know what to do. I was, I suppose, hallucinating. During our last conversation, I even heard Sukesh's voice! I could hear his voice in the background, speaking to her children. What? Is Sukesh in Mumbai with his sister? Is my mind playing tricks on me? But this doubt took root, as it was my only hope now. I had never considered this angle. How else could a man disappear into thin air? Is he there with his sister in Mumbai? By now, I understood their ways, that they had all sorts of games up their sleeves. This doubt grew stronger within me. I could not go to Mumbai as I was in my third month of pregnancy.

As I pondered what to do, I stumbled upon one of Sukesh's niece's phone numbers. She was about 16 years old and used to linger around me whenever they visited from Mumbai to Udupi. She chatted incessantly like any other teenager and lived in the same apartment complex. I had to take the risk, so I rang her up.

I asked her, "Is your uncle (my husband) in Mumbai at your aunt's (Sukesh's sister) house?" She replied casually, 'Yes,' and I was stunned! My legs began to tremble, and I thought I was going to faint. She said, "He's been there for nearly a week. They aren't allowing him to leave the house. Aunty locks the door when she goes out. I don't know why."

Stunned by this information, I steadied my quavering voice, suppressing all my pent-up emotions, and asked her, "Could you please do me a favour? Whenever you go there, could you ask him to call me? I need to speak with him. I'm completely in the dark about what's happening. Please help me. Be careful with this so you don't get into trouble." She agreed.

I remained unconvinced; however, I hoped that Sukesh was indeed at his sister's house. I couldn't make any sense of it. When did he come to India? Why is he in Mumbai? And why is he at the house of a sister with whom he no longer wishes to converse? What was he doing there? What's so secret about it? Why didn't he reach out to me or inform me? Why aren't they allowing him to leave the house? Is he in some trouble? Or is this some grand scheme of his family? Are they involved in a systematic fleecing operation targeting girls from poor backgrounds? A multitude of stories began to form in my mind.

My phone rang the next morning, and so did my heart. It was an unknown number. I hoped it was Sukesh calling.

"____" I received the call and didn't say anything.

"Hello...." it was him! I immediately burst into tears.

"Hello...." I was choking. I couldn't breathe. I sat down, leaning against the wall. I panicked. My eyes were welling up, and I was struggling to catch my breath. The phone slipped out of my hand and fell.

"Hey... are you there... can you hear me?"

"Haaa…. Haaaaaaaaaa…." Suddenly, I gasped. I took a deep breath and began to cry. There was no one at home. Amma had gone to the fields, my sister was at school, and Grandpa must be loitering about somewhere. I just held my belly to check if everything was alright.

After a long, harrowing minute, I looked around for my phone and picked it up at once. Still crying silently, I said, "Hello…."

It seemed he was in a hurry to speak with me. He said, "I can't talk to you much right now. I'm calling from a public booth. I truly apologise. I'll come and explain everything to you. I have to listen to these people now. Don't worry, I'm not going to leave you. Please be patient. I love you. Don't mention to them that I've called. Give me a couple of days. I'll either come or call you. Just take care. I can't talk for long; I have to rush back. Bye."

That's it! The call disconnected. I let out a sigh of relief. At last, I knew where he was and that he was alive after all. I waited in vain for his calls over the next two weeks.

The Rise and Fall of Reconciliation

One fine day, his sister, who lived in Udupi, called me. "Hey, Sukesh is coming here tomorrow; you can meet him." I did not have the patience to even question her. They had taken it for granted that I knew Sukesh's whereabouts, and it seemed they didn't care much. What a fraud I had gotten myself into!

I couldn't sleep the whole night. They had asked me to arrive at 10 am. I was there at 9:30 am. As I entered her flat on the third floor, his sister opened the door for me. I could see Sukesh sitting on the sofa in a corner. His sister from Mumbai was there too. I stood next to the kitchen door with my arms crossed. I was so angry that I didn't look at his face. This was a moment of truth for me. I was also grappling with a bit of guilt as we had both left home without informing anyone, and this was the first time I had met his family since then.

One of the sisters began, "Alright, let's leave them alone. Let them talk to each other." Then they went into one of the bedrooms. Sukesh rose from the sofa, walking slowly beside me. I didn't even glance at his face. I was clenching my teeth and looking down sideways at the floor. He attempted to touch my crossed arm. I was about to erupt, but I somehow controlled myself and pushed his hands away. He moved closer again, touching my shoulder with both arms. By now, I was fuming. I shrugged his hand off my shoulder and pointed my index finger at him, my eyes wide open and trembling with anger. Words wouldn't come out of my mouth. With his hands folded, he stepped back and said, "I'm sorry, dear, I'm sorry."

I turned my face away from him. I was furious. He continuously begged me to forgive him. I still didn't look at his face.

Finally, I met his gaze and, with a controlled, trembling voice, asked him a barrage of questions.

What happened in Dubai?

"My friend fell in the bathroom and died. That's why I had to wind up the business and return. I was arrested at Dubai airport due to mistaken identification."

How did you get out?

"After a week, they released me once they realised, they had arrested the wrong person."

How did you end up in Mumbai?

"My sister asked me to come to Mumbai after my release."

Why didn't you contact me when you were released or when you arrived in Mumbai?

"My sister told me that you were very anxious and hence not to contact you. She asked me to come to Mumbai post which I could speak to you. She booked my flight ticket."

What's your financial arrangement with your sister?

"As you know, my elder sister is involved in the money-lending business in Mumbai. I hadn't repaid the loan I took from her. She asked me to work in Mumbai and repay what I owe her."

None of what he said—nothing at all—made any sense. I was not in the mood to interrogate further. It was highly probable that all this was a lie. Perhaps that day, when I dropped him at Bangalore airport, he never flew to Saudi at all? Maybe he went straight to Mumbai.

After a few hours, we had lunch in the sombre atmosphere. I didn't know how much of what Sukesh had said was credible. But given my situation, I simply had to go with the flow. I had no money, I was married, I was pregnant, and I couldn't stay long with Amma. My husband was jobless, and I was jobless myself.

There was absolute silence between us. He sat in the corner chair, his head hung low. What an actor! Or was he? Was he telling the truth? No… I was not prepared to give him the benefit of the doubt. There were so many loose ends that I was certain this was a setup. After a few more minutes of awkward silence, his sisters began conversing. The younger one, who lived in Udupi, had an offer for us. She asked us to manage her paying guest accommodations (PG). She had two PGs: one for boys and one for girls. She said we could both have a job. By all accounts, I knew it was a trap, but I had no other option for the time being.

I immediately agreed and said, "Please pay me for my work. I desperately need a job as I have no cash on me." I was frightened she was asking us to work to pay off the money my husband owed them. She agreed to pay me, though she didn't disclose how much. Nor was I in a position to ask her how much she was going to pay. For me, a job and money were crucial, and her offer was exactly what I needed.

The job was set to start the very next day. Now, the more significant challenge was to go home and convince Amma. What was I going to tell her? By then, she was pressuring me to separate from my husband. She was convinced that Sukesh and his family were out to ruin me. But I had to take my chances. I went home, told Amma everything, packed my things, and returned the next morning after much persuasion.

I was staying in the girls' PG, where I had a room to myself. There were ten girls in the PG. The PG didn't have a separate building; three houses were rented in an apartment complex. The rates for the rooms were fixed depending on whether the girls were sharing or wanted a room to themselves. Meals were provided. The same situation applied to the boys' PG, which was located in another apartment complex a few blocks down the road, where there were eight boys.

My role was to cook for everyone and manage the administration for all eighteen of them. I had a helper who assisted me. I had to prepare meals for all of them. The girls were served in the building where I stayed, but I had to transport food to the nearby boys' hostel in large lunch boxes along with my helper. Thus, food had to be transferred daily from the girls' PG to the boys' PG, covering three meals a day: breakfast, lunch, and dinner.

Sukesh was appointed as the caretaker in the boys' PG. Sukesh did not have a mobile phone, so we were left without contact. We were prohibited from being in touch with one another and strictly forbidden from seeing each other, even when I visited the boys' hostel. One day, I asked one of the boys from the PG for his mobile number so I could speak to Sukesh. I was not in a position to argue or fight. My younger sister-in-law was, however, rather good to me. She took good care of me, looking after my food, accommodation, blood tests, tablets, and so on during my pregnancy.

After a month, I felt an urge to see my mother. I requested two days off. I called Sukesh and informed him that I was returning home to Bejjolli for a day or two. He began pleading with me to take him along, expressing that he wanted to talk to me. However, they were unlikely to let him go. I asked his sister to send him with me, but she flatly refused. I understood that he was feeling down, and I was, too. On my way to the bus stand, I stopped by the boys' PG and told him they were refusing to send him. I advised Sukesh to stay behind, assuring him that I would be back soon. What a compulsory situation we found ourselves in. The sisters whom he raised, supported financially, and watched get married were the ones controlling his life—and mine— now. I, a fiercely independent girl who never yielded to threats throughout my life, was caught in such a compromising position.

I arrived home in Bejjolli around 10 am. In a farming household, rest is a foreign concept. All family members are constantly engaged in some form of work. Pregnancy is no excuse. In our village communities, it is believed that being physically active during pregnancy is beneficial and aids in delivery. While city dwellers spend money on yoga and other classes, we are compelled to stay active. I commenced with the household chores.

I was mopping the floor at noon when I heard the sound of an auto-rickshaw approaching. Villages are quite serene during noon, except for the buzzing insects and the occasional bird chirpings. The approach of any vehicle can be heard from afar. Curious about who had arrived, I went to the back of the house and peered through the window. Sukesh was getting out of the auto! Alone!

I was rooted to the spot for a few seconds before I composed myself and headed to the main door. He had arrived without any luggage. I asked, "Why have you come? Did you inform your sister or come without telling them?"

Before he could respond, my phone rang; it was his sister. She began shouting, "What's wrong with him? He's acting like a mentally disturbed person. We've sent him to you. Has he come?"

I said, "Yes… but…"

"Click." She disconnected.

He had not paid for the auto fare. The driver came in search of him. I paid the auto driver and sent him off. Sukesh walked straight inside the house and sat in a chair. He was not in his senses; he was acting strangely. He looked deranged and was mumbling to himself. Neither he nor I had any idea what he was talking about.

I offered him a glass of water, which he gulped down in one go, spilling much of it on his shirt. He was a well-built man with a chest full of hair. With his shirt unbuttoned at the top, an untrimmed beard, and a water-soaked chest, he resembled an Indian movie villain. Much contrary to his appearance, I knew he had a soft heart within.

I sat next to him, rubbing his back. I had a child on the way, and I felt like I needed to care for another child—just that this one was a grown-up.

"Are you hungry? Would you like to have lunch?"

He didn't respond; he had been staring at the floor for half an hour. I went into the kitchen and brought some rice mixed with fish curry. I had seen him like this when he was drunk; his mother would feed him. Only today, he was not drunk. I began to feed him.

Just then, Amma returned from the paddy fields. With the areca hat still perched upon her head, drenched in sweat, the lower edge of her saree and petticoat was raised to knee length and knotted around her waist. Her bare legs were still wet from the clay in the field. She stared at Sukesh and then at me. In that ten-second gaze, the entire data transferred from my mother's head to mine. I looked back at her, giving a silent, helpless look.

Amma went wild upon seeing him. She began shouting, "You've ruined my girl's life." I rushed to Amma and held her back. Tears of anguish streamed down her face. I don't recall seeing her in this state before, not even when Pappa passed away. I said to Amma, "It seems he is experiencing some sort of mental trauma. Let's not worsen the situation. Let's wait for a while." She shot me a hard look and walked off to wash herself.

Given our precarious financial situation, my husband's arrival was an additional mouth to feed and to make matters worse, he appeared to be losing his mind. I felt devastated, broken, and drained. How much can a human endure? But I had to. There was a new life growing inside me now. I had to live for that life. None of this was the fault of the new life developing within me.

My first concern now was to get Sukesh straightened out. I wanted to consult a psychiatrist, but we had no money. We were financially broke, living hand-to-mouth. Nor could we tell anyone about our situation in the village; it would be a shame for us. Who could I share my problems with? So many friends and relatives contributed to my marriage. How could I tell them that I had married such a man and that now my situation was this? I was already indebted to them all and was not in a position to ask for further help.

I had to quit the PG job. From the day I came home, I could not return. I couldn't leave him alone at home. My Amma was acting half mad; she shouted at him whenever she saw him. He, on the other hand, always seemed lost. He rarely spoke and had his food on time. Other than that, he was confined to one corner of the veranda while my grandfather occupied the other corner. His mental state showed extreme fluctuations. One fine day, he would start speaking and making sense; the next day, he would be completely withdrawn.

My younger sister was being affected by all this drama. She even disclosed, "I don't want to get married at all in life. I'm scared that I, too, will end up with such a husband." I used to pacify her by saying not all men are like that; it was my bad luck to have to go through this. I assured her that I would get her married to the best man in the world. All I asked was for her to focus on her studies so she could go out into the world and find a good job and a better life. Deep down, I wished she would find a man of her choosing rather than us setting her up with someone.

Sharanya, younger than me by five years, in contrast, was perhaps the luckiest of the three of us. She wasn't fully aware of most of our struggles; by the time she began attending high school, both her elder sisters had been married off, and a support system was already in place. She had plenty of dresses to wear throughout her university years, unlike the rest of us. We had to manage with only two sets of Salwar Kameez [17] for the entire year. During the monsoon season, it gets wet and does not dry off due to high humidity. We ended up wearing the damp ones.

Being the youngest, she had a relatively more straightforward life than we did, although she faced her own struggles. She completed her Diploma in Electronics Engineering and secured a job in Bangalore, our state's capital city. Things improved somewhat for my Amma after my sister moved to Bangalore.

---

17. Salwar Kameez: Salwar Kameez is a long tunic with a loose-fitting pant worn by women in India.

She earned a decent salary and could afford to send money to my Amma after covering her expenses. There was now a flow of cash into the house.

They say that when girls from smaller towns move to larger cities, their behaviour shifts due to newfound freedom and exposure to various vices. However, I didn't notice much difference in Sharanya, except perhaps in how she dressed. During her college years, she would wear nothing other than a Salwar Kameez. The only change I observed in her after moving to Bangalore was that she began wearing modern, stylish clothes, particularly Western ones, and looked beautiful.

She fell in love with a boy from our community who worked alongside her at the same company. We arranged their marriage, and they are now settled in Bangalore.

A month passed, and as usual, Amma taunted Sukesh whenever she walked past him. He responded by asking her not to torment him with her words. He promised to bounce back and do something, which was a surprising development.

Since his sisters had confiscated his mobile phone, he was unable to contact anyone. All his contacts were stored on the phone, and he did not know any numbers by heart. I asked Amma to leave him alone so he could think things through and get out of this depression. He was wavering, fluctuating between stability and instability. When he was stable, he made sense, and when he wasn't, he spoke nonsense.

One day, while in his right mind, he stated he would go to Udupi and meet the family of his friend who was in Saudi Arabia to obtain a few phone numbers to contact them. He borrowed money from me, which I had to get from Amma. Looking at my situation, I had no choice but to see the optimistic side of everything. Otherwise, I had no reason to be alive. It was getting dark, and he still hadn't returned. He had taken my mobile phone so that I could reach him, yet he wouldn't answer my calls. Finally, he picked up.

"Hello… where are you?"

"Madam," said a stranger's voice, "Madam, how do you know this man?"

"He's, my husband. Why? What has happened? Is he alright? Where is he?

"Madam, your husband is drunk and not in his right mind. He is lying on the table here. Please arrange to take him home, or we must call the police."

"No… No… please. I'll arrange to get him home. Please give me half an hour. Thank you very much." I noted down the name and address of the place he was in.

I didn't know what to do. There was no way I could go and fetch him in the darkness. There was no bridge across the river to our village. We had to cross by boat or take the longer route by road. As a last resort, I had to request some neighbourhood boys I had grown up with to go and collect him. They were all in for a shock. They were angry with me for not having told them about this. It was exceedingly humiliating to disclose anything to anyone in the village. You know how rumours spread. Eventually, they brought him home late at night, and it became the headline of the village the next day.

We had to confine him at home and not allow him out alone. I sometimes had to force him to eat while assisting Amma with the household chores. Due to my pregnancy, I could not help much in the fields, and Amma also seemed to have resigned herself to fate. She never spoke to Sukesh and didn't even acknowledge his presence, walking right past him instead.

One fine day, while I was feeding him, he suddenly recalled his friend's phone number in Saudi Arabia. He immediately called him on my phone and had a chat. I was at a loss for words; one moment, he seemed lost, and the next, he was back to his senses. He chatted for a while, but I could not overhear the conversation. I was more worried about my mobile currency depleting due to the international call. He returned with a gleaming look on his face, appearing very happy. His friend began calling him daily. Sukesh requested a Visa from him, and his friend even sent him some money. Sukesh mentioned that his friend was soon opening a supermarket and wanted Sukesh to come over to look after it. Did I believe him? No! I had resigned myself to my fate by now, having had similar experiences with him.

Ray of Hope

The tickets arrived, and his departure date was set. Did he have any money with him? No. I had to pawn the last piece of jewellery I owned, the essence, the identity of a married woman, my *Karimani/ Mangalsutra* [18], and send him off.

In April, I was in my sixth month of pregnancy. I was clinging to a ray of hope, wishing for him to get back on track. He called me every week, and I told him how very happy I was for him. After a month, he also sent me some money. At least I didn't have to beg anyone for money now. My husband could finally afford the expenses. I was so glad but cautious about celebrating. He mentioned that he worked for a supermarket in Saudi Arabia. Thanks to the money he sent regularly, I could save some to retrieve my Karimani/Mangalsutra.

It was July, and my delivery date was approaching. One night, I began to feel uneasy. The following morning, Amma and I went to the Udupi Government Maternity Hospital. After the check-up, the lady doctor asked me

---

18. Karimani/Mangalsutra: A chain made in gold with black beads considered to be auspicious of a married woman in India.

to get admitted immediately, stating that I could deliver at any moment. This time, at least I had money in hand for the hospital expenses, so that was taken care of. I was neither anxious nor fearful about the delivery; my other stresses in life felt far more overwhelming. I even approached the duty nurses and asked them to induce labour pain by administering injections. Honestly, I may sound sexist, but I longed for a male child as I was weary of being a girl. So did my Amma; she was tired of raising three of her daughters, a daughter of my elder sister and a daughter of my aunt. It was only natural for her to want me to have a baby boy. However, Sukesh wanted a girl child. We live in a matriarchal society in this region, where our lineage is passed down through the girls. Hence, having a daughter in the family was deemed very important, unlike the preference for a male child in other regions of the country. On July 17th, I delivered. When the doctor informed me that I had delivered a girl, I exclaimed, "Ohh, a girl?"

"Why do you say that?" the doctor replied, "She's such a cutie." When I tell my daughter now, she pretends to be angry. Sukesh spoke to me before the delivery, and until I went into the labour room, he kept insisting it would be a girl. He was very pleased. We stayed in the hospital for two more days. The baby was healthy, albeit slightly underweight. Sukesh was on cloud nine, quite literally! No celebrations, no balloons, no cakes, no cradle event, nothing of the sort, as I was not in a position for any extravagance. We named her *Saarika*. Sukesh sent money to buy a gold chain for the baby. He seemed settled into his new role. It was somewhat hard for me to believe that things were falling into place after all that we had experienced. He used to send dresses and dolls for the baby from Saudi Arabia with people coming to Udupi. He had yet to meet the baby.

I was still unemployed. Caring for the baby was my full-time job. I partially repaid the loans from my marriage with whatever Sukesh sent. Yes, I missed Sukesh a great deal. Yet, I was happy for him and us. Happy for him as he wasn't drinking there. Happy for us as money was coming in. I knew he wasn't drinking; I could tell from his voice. I had heard that drinking alcohol is illegal in Saudi Arabia.

Year by:

It was Saarika's first birthday. A year had already passed. The sea of life was calm, with no storms in sight. It felt somewhat surreal for me. We had a very low-key birthday celebration at home. I made a video call to Sukesh. He was thrilled, as he had wished for a daughter, and there she was. However, Saarika had not yet seen her Pappa, except through video calls. She couldn't respond much to the video calls. Sukesh said, "Let's celebrate her second birthday in Saudi." He mentioned he was working on bringing us over. I was excited. He said, "I'll arrange a visiting visa for you both. Just bring your study certificates along. Perhaps you can look for a job here."

He seemed happy. He wasn't drinking and was working hard. I also believed it was better to be with him there. I don't think I ever had a desire to go abroad, but now, I just wanted to be with him. I wanted to be like any other normal couple, staying together with our child and leading a normal life. I started dreaming about how I would take care of my husband and child, how I would manage the house, cook for my husband, look forward to his return from work in the evening, and greet him with a smile. I imagined how he would play with Saarika and how happy she would be to have her Pappa around to look after her. We could go out on weekends and so forth. My dream bubble was growing, and I just hoped it wouldn't burst.

Things finally seemed uneventful. He was so fond of his daughter that he asked me to send a photo of Saarika every day. Video calls were challenging as the mobile signal strength in our village was too weak for them to go through. He had also collected all the photos on a pen drive. During this time, there was bridge construction work happening over the river Suvarna, which would significantly reduce our commute time to the nearest town, eliminating our dependency on the boatman. However, I felt bad for the boatman, whose livelihood would be greatly affected. In general, this would be of great benefit to the surrounding villages, which is why they had constructed two mud roads for easy crossing. My sister spoke to Sukesh at that time, saying, "*Jeeju* [19], everyone around has two-wheelers at home, but we don't. We have to go by auto and wait for the bus." Sukesh immediately sent money to her to buy a scooter. Sometimes, he can be overwhelming in his generosity. We purchased a second-hand scooter for our commutes. I was not very keen, though, as it was a substantial investment for us. But my sister always had her way.

Amma wasn't very happy about me going to Saudi Arabia, especially with a child to look after. She was too wary of Sukesh and his waywardness, having lost faith in him. I wasn't particularly pleased about staying with my Amma simply because I didn't want to be a

---

19. Jeeja/Jeeju: Brother-in-law in Hindi language.

burden on her. Even after getting married, if I had to stay with her, then what was the point of marrying? On the other hand, I looked forward to a normal married life with my husband and daughter.

I wished for a good education for my daughter and hoped she wouldn't have to struggle as I did, going through what I experienced to become educated. Somehow, the fire within me was so strong that I knew the only way out of our poverty was to empower myself through education.

We sisters were fortunate to be born in a generation where girls were encouraged to pursue education. In contrast, in my Amma's generation, it was uncommon for girls to attend school. My Amma never had the opportunity to go to school. My parents could not afford to send us to fancy private or English medium schools. The only school we could afford to go to was the government-run vernacular Kannada medium school[20]. We had to walk 5 km daily to the nearest primary

20. Kannada medium school: Kannada is the state language of Karnataka. The students have a choice to choose the medium of instruction. Either Kannada or English.

school. The entire village's kids would walk together to the school. Starting with the first group, each household would add on to the kids as they passed each house. For most kids in the village, the mid-day meal [21] was the only main attraction. Many children used to attend school for this very reason. This was an incentive provided by the government to encourage children to go to school. Local village children were otherwise hesitant to attend. This offered parents a chance for some peace at home and allowed the children some enjoyable time.

After school, for my 11th and 12th grades, I joined the government arts college in Udupi, which was quite far from our home and required commuting by bus. I performed reasonably well in my studies, and my grades were decent. After completing 12th grade, I wished to enrol in a General Nursing course. However, our financial situation did not

---

21. Mid-day meal: A scheme introduced by the state government to encourage kids from poor financial backgrounds to attend schools and also induce nutrition into their diet by providing boiled egg with the meal.

allow me to afford a private institution. I attempted to gain admission to the government nursing college but to no avail. I was even called for counselling, yet they required us to deposit an initial amount for the seat, which was far beyond our means. I felt very disappointed at that time. With no other options, I opted to join the DMLT (Diploma in Medical Lab Technician) course. The fee was ₹20,000 per year, which at that time was an astronomical amount for us to pay; thus, we applied for an education loan at a bank.

I was an art student with no background in science. In the first year, I found it quite difficult to cope with new subjects and terminologies. It was a three-year course. During the first year, my Pappa fell ill and was admitted to the hospital. Unfortunately, he didn't survive, leaving my world devoid of a male presence to care for us. Left behind were my Amma, my two sisters, and me, along with my aged grandfather. Though financially, it didn't make much difference to us, the moral support of a male member possibly weighed on our minds. Now, the four of us women were left at home. My Amma was a very strong lady, or perhaps circumstances made us all strong. There was a will to survive. I didn't know how, but we had to survive. Selling milk became our major source of income. I was attending college while my younger sister was in high school. Amma gave me ₹10 daily. The bus ticket cost ₹7, and the remaining ₹3 was to be returned to her in the evening. College was a mix of emotions. It was a fantastic learning experience, but our financial situation weighed heavily on us. At times, I couldn't afford the exam fees of ₹450. My friends in college pooled their money to help cover it.

Finally, the tickets and the visa arrived for Saarika and me to fly off to Saudi Arabia. His friend in Mangalore had arranged the visa and tickets for us. I had never travelled on an aeroplane before. The closest I had been to one was when they occasionally flew in the sky above my house. When we were young, we used to lie down in the dry paddy fields whenever we spotted one flying overhead and watch the entire path the aircraft took. Sometimes, we would all shout together, thinking someone on the plane might hear us. Such a naïve, carefree life it was. We were so happy in our childhood. How complicated things become as we grow up! In the pursuit of preparing for life, which ironically is supposed to be happier, we get lost in chasing materialism and complicated relationships. It's a mad race, for God knows what. In the process, we lose all the happiness accumulated in our childhood. Now, we seek ways to regain that happiness we once had, the happiness we grew up with and gradually lost. I'm being philosophical now.

Setting aside flying on an aeroplane, I had never travelled outside my home state. I hadn't even travelled by train. And here I was, flying on an aeroplane to an unknown country. It was the 15th of August 2016. The country was celebrating Independence Day. My Amma and two sisters came to Mangalore airport to see us off. My younger sister was very excited as if she were flying instead of me. My Amma was inconsolable, shedding tears non-stop for two hours, all the way from our house to the airport. My elder sister was also very emotional. With all this, naturally, I had tears streaming down my face. I just hugged them all and bid farewell. Saarika didn't know what was happening; she was perhaps too young to understand it all.

Was I scared? I wasn't scared at all. I think we small-town kids are genetically wired to be brave. Moreover, I was so fed up with life that I needed an escape. I wished to live separately with Sukesh. I felt I had suffered too much until now. Sukesh, too, was saying, enough of India. Let's live in Saudi forever. It was a kind of dream to me. I wanted to have a good life with my husband and daughter.

Our first flight was from Mangalore to Mumbai. From Mumbai, we had to catch an international flight to Riyadh. We checked in, and the flight took off from Mangalore at 6:00 pm. I was excited to see the inside of an aeroplane for the first time. All these days, I had wondered how they could fly so high with so many people on board. And today, I was in that aircraft myself. Perhaps it will pass over my village. Will I be able to identify it by looking out of the window?

The most novel experience I had was the boat in my village. It was a novelty because I wonder how many get to experience it, even as a one-off event. For us, it was a daily routine to cross the river in the boat. The maximum number of people the boat could hold was about ten, and the furthest we travelled was about 500 metres across the river's breadth. And here I was, sitting in something that flies through the air, seating hundreds of them, carrying us hundreds of miles away.

The air hostesses were quite pretty. Until now, I had only seen them in advertisements. However, seeing them in person, they were even more attractive. One of them, noticing me carrying Saarika, took the hand baggage from me and guided me to our middle seat, much to my disappointment. As I mentioned, courage was ingrained in us small-town girls. I asked the gentleman beside me, who occupied the window seat if we could swap seats, as this was the first flight of my life. He agreed without any hesitation. I was thrilled to be seated by the window. I could see the long wing of the aircraft outside the window and wondered if it could support the weight of such a massive machine.

Saarika had to sit on my lap. The gentleman who swapped seats with me was kind enough to help me with my seat belt. I did not know how to lock or unlock it. I listened attentively to the instructions given by the air hostess. Looking around, I noticed many people were not paying attention. I felt like the most studious student in class, absorbing every word from the teacher's mouth. If there had been a surprise quiz, I would have aced it.

I could see outside the window and was showing Saarika the other parked aircraft. Our plane was moving slowly towards the runway. We spotted an aircraft taking off a little distance from us at that moment. I wondered what all those alphanumeric symbols meant, written on the signboards scattered across the ground. There were lights of various sizes and colours. The aircraft came to a halt. The air hostesses had finished checking everyone's seatbelts and upright seat positions. The engine noise began to grow louder. Suddenly, the aircraft lurched forward at great speed, and I gripped the seat handles tightly. It continued speeding along the ground. I wondered why it wasn't flying yet. I had heard that the Mangalore airstrip wasn't very long. A few years ago, there was a mishap when an aircraft overshot the airstrip and fell into the gorge.

All of a sudden, I felt a sinking sensation in my stomach. We were in the air! We were flying! I could see the buildings below. As it grew darker but not completely dark, I could see clusters of yellow lights below. I could also see roads and vehicles moving on them. The sight was beautiful. How lucky were the birds? They witnessed this view daily from above.

My ears popped. Saarika was eager to look out of the window as well. The sun had already set, but the skyline remained crimson. After a while, the aircraft seemed to have stabilised. Saarika was feeling sleepy and dozed off in my lap. The seatbelt sign was switched off, and the lights came on. The air hostesses were bustling about, asking if anyone needed refreshments. I had read online that the food was costly on the flight. However, I was thirsty and requested some water. The hostess handed me a small bottle of water. I inquired about the cost, and she said it was free. I smiled back at her and finished the water in one gulp. I needed another bottle but hesitated to ask. I stared vacantly out the window, trying to replay the events from the day of my marriage to this moment. Phew… What a journey!

I heard the loud sound of a beep and an announcement by the pilot. I woke up. We were about to land in Mumbai. I had dozed off for a good hour or so. I could see a large cluster of golden lights in the distance. It must be the city of Mumbai. We were asked to fasten our seatbelts. I had never removed mine. I tried to wake Saarika, but she was not in the mood. I let it be as the lights in the cabin went off. I could see the cluster of lights again in the distance. This view was so beautiful. The earth looked calm and peaceful. Possibly, that's why they say heaven is in the sky. Once you touch down, all the problems seem to come rushing back.

Again, I started feeling that familiar sensation in my stomach. For some reason, my ears were in a lot of pain. Finally, I realised that the aircraft had touched down, as there were numerous vibrations and thuds. With the speed at which it travelled on the ground, I wondered if it would ever stop. To my relief, the aircraft finally came to a standstill. The seatbelt sign was still on, but people had already gotten up to retrieve their luggage. Why is everyone in such a hurry? I, the studious student, did not budge from my seat. By this time, Saarika had woken up too.

I whispered to her, "We are in Mumbaaaaai!" even though it didn't seem to matter to her. Still, I felt compelled to share my excitement with someone.

I had to catch the connecting international flight from a different terminal. The flight was at 12:30 AM, and it was already 7:30 pm. We were hungry, but I was rushing to reach the international terminal. Upon enquiring, I was directed to take the shuttle bus to the international terminal as there was no internal connection. The bus took almost 45 minutes to arrive. I grabbed a quick bite at the prohibitively expensive restaurant inside the airport, and after all the formalities, we were finally on our way to Saudi Arabia.

This was a huge aircraft with an abundance of seats. Isn't it amazing to think about? Hundreds of people are transported safely by air to far-off destinations. Fortunately, at the check-in counter, they had allocated me a seat with ample legroom as I was travelling with a child. It was yet another short flight of four hours, and we arrived in Riyadh at 4:40 AM Indian Standard Time as I glanced at my wristwatch. While disembarking, I noticed the time on the clock at the airport, which showed 2:10 AM. I was a couple of hours younger. That's pleasant, I thought. I messaged Sukesh to let him know we had landed. I was carrying an international roaming SIM card from India and was eager to see Sukesh. I could also understand his excitement as he was meeting his daughter in person for the first time.

Disembarking from the plane, it hardly felt like I had arrived in a foreign country. Everywhere I looked, I could see only Indians—or people who resembled Indians. The women were all clad in Burqas. Sukesh had already informed me about women's compulsory wearing of the Burqa in Saudi Arabia. I had bought a Burqa in Udupi itself. The shopkeeper wasn't overly surprised when a non-Muslim woman requested a Burqa, mentioning that it was common for him. The salesgirl in his shop helped me find the right size of Burqa.

I proceeded to the washroom and asked one of the women to hold Saarika, who was fast asleep. I freshened up and quickly donned the Burqa over my dress. It felt rather strange. I often wondered how women felt inside the Burqa when I saw them wearing it in my hometown, enduring the region's sweltering heat. It was awkward for me, but the view was quite clear through the netted face cover. I just hoped Saarika wouldn't wake up and start crying at the sight of me. I pondered how Sukesh would recognise me.

As Saarika was asleep, I had to carry her. I picked up a trolley and asked for assistance to lift the bag from the conveyor belt onto the trolley. I struggled to push the trolley while carrying Saarika, but somehow, I reached the exit. There he was, waiting for us. I waved at him excitedly, but I hadn't realised he couldn't see the biggest grin of my life under the burqa. Oh my God, how relieved I was to see him! He picked Saarika off my shoulders, but she wouldn't let go of me, even in her sleep. He took the trolley from me, allowing Saarika to cling to me.

I could see through the nets, even in the artificial light. He was beaming with delight, and so was I. He said we needed to take another flight from there to a city called

Tabuk. We boarded an airport transfer bus. After a brief 10-minute ride, we arrived at the domestic terminal. Sukesh and I chatted non-stop, as there was much catching up to do.

We spent a few hours in the domestic terminal as our flight was at 6:15 am. In the meantime, Saarika woke from her nap. She refused to approach Sukesh, as she had met him for the first time. Sukesh had bought her a small teddy bear. She took it from his hands but was hesitant to get closer. Sukesh was keen to hold her—his daughter—but it seemed she was still evaluating him. Finally, we arrived at Tabuk airport at 8:30 am, and I was utterly exhausted.

Life in the Desert

Sukesh had told me that Tabuk was a relatively small town, but it appeared to be a beautiful city. It was so clean, with well-laid roads, streetlights, and lovely buildings all around. We drove directly to a serviced apartment, which I adored. The flat was furnished, and I was in awe of the kitchen; I had never seen such a stunning kitchen before. It had a lovely view of the street in front. I collapsed onto the super-soft bed. By this time, Saarika felt comfortable with Sukesh, and I had fallen asleep within moments.

We were in the service apartment for a month, and after that, we moved into the new rented flat near his partner Moosa's house. Sukesh was managing the service station of a local Saudi man named Moosa. I wasn't sure if that was his actual name, but that's how Sukesh referred to him. As is typical in Saudi Arabia and much of the Middle East, expats cannot own a business without a local partner, who is known as *Kafeel*. I didn't know much about Moosa; I only knew that Sukesh was operating a vehicle service centre alongside him. I never deemed it important to know too many details about his dealings.

At first, I felt pretty bored as Sukesh came home late at night. It wasn't very interesting at home. Cooking and other household tasks were my only pastimes. Yes, there was a TV, and we could receive Indian channels, but I was never inclined to watch those soaps for some reason. Saarika ended up watching her favourite cartoons most of the time. I had a knack for cooking Mangalorean cuisine and would try dishes according to Sukesh's taste.

I wasn't stepping out of the house because I had to wear a burqa. I wasn't comfortable in it; it felt claustrophobic, and I wasn't used to it. We could go to the nearby park, but having to wear a burqa discouraged me. Later, Sukesh cajoled me into going along to see the city. Over time, I grew accustomed to the burqa, which was convenient—I could wear any ordinary dress underneath. All I had to do was put on a burqa over it and then go out, not worrying about make-up. I never saw a local lady's face while there; everyone was covered with a burqa, making it impossible to recognise anyone except for the male accompanying them.

Gradually, I grew to like the place. There was an area called Sharalam, bustling with Keralites[22]. We could

----

22. Keralites: a native or inhabitant of the southwestern Indian state of Kerala.

find everything Indian there; it became our go-to spot for shopping, particularly for Indian spices. The meat was inexpensive, which was fantastic because I adored meat, and so did Sukesh and Saarika. I experimented with numerous dishes, drawing inspiration from YouTube. Although many fruits and vegetables were imported, they appeared and tasted fresh. Sukesh cajoled Saarika by buying her dolls, ice creams, and chocolates. Slowly and steadily, she started to like him to the extent that she didn't want him to go away to work.

Sukesh would leave at 9 am and return by 1:30 pm. Due to the hot climate, people don't venture out in the afternoons. He would leave again at 4:00 pm and return only by 11:00 or 12:00 late at night. Sometimes, Sukesh would take Saarika in the morning and bring her back at noon. That was a lovely bonding time for father and daughter. While Sukesh didn't have a fixed weekly day off, he was flexible about taking days off. On those days, we would go out together. We were a typical happy family. Touch wood. These were the days I had been looking forward to since marriage. How turbulent have the days been until now?

Rewind Mode – The Great Indian Wedding Circus

Indeed, the wedding feels like a circus. There are numerous aspects, characters, nuances, politics, juggling, drama, risks, rehearsals, performances, and jesters. After a brief initial courtship period, with both families agreeing to the relationship, everything was set in motion, and we needed to convey this to my paternal uncles and close relatives. Some of them were in a better financial position, while we, in contrast, were leading a hand-to-mouth existence. My Amma informed some of them about the alliance and discussed the way forward. They matched the horoscopes, and everything looked fine. We weren't considering an engagement ceremony due to the apparent desire to avoid expenses. However, the groom's side insisted on having one. We didn't have any funds. Where could we possibly find money for an engagement? My brother-in-law and uncles came together and helped us a little. But there were still some expenses to consider, such as purchasing a saree and a gold ring. Where would we procure the money for that? I had completed the lab technician course with great difficulty, financed through an educational loan of ₹60,000 from the bank. I struggled to repay this amount from my salary, let alone afford a gold ring. But what must be, must be. Only the bare minimum of shopping was undertaken with great caution.

Engagement

In my parents' time, an engagement ceremony was a very private affair in our community. Often, even the bride and groom were absent. It was more of two families coming together than just the two individuals. If the families are okay with each other, the bride and the groom had no say. The family elders would exchange betel leaves and betel nuts, both revered as symbols of good fortune. Then came the concept of exchanging rings, cutting an engagement cake, customs rooted in Western culture, and using neutrally decorated venues.

To start the process, a venue in a hotel was finalised and booked, with a minimum number of people being invited from both sides.

One of Sukesh's three sisters was a beautician. I could not afford a beautician for the engagement, but his sister offered to take care of my make-up for the ceremony. She requested that I arrive at the venue earlier and assured me she would take full responsibility for my make-up. It was a relief for me as it meant one less expense. I told Amma that Sukesh's sister had offered to help, and Amma was glad she was getting me married into a good family, as they were so mindful of her daughter.

On D-day, we arrived early at the engagement hall, waiting for his sister to come and do my makeup. Although I have never had any makeup applied to me before, I believe it's an innate desire for a girl to want to look beautiful. Out of nowhere, this desire suddenly sparked excitement within me. I want to look radiant on this special occasion. Who wouldn't appreciate some special attention?

It had been an hour since Amma, my sisters, and I had arrived. Sukesh's sister was nowhere to be seen. We tried calling her, but she did not answer. The phone was ringing. We consoled ourselves by saying she must be on her way. Time was running out, and I felt anxious. Everyone around me was anxious. All I had on was the saree and jewellery. We couldn't waste any more time; we had to get on with it. Who carries a makeup kit on such occasions? With her missing, my sisters had to make do with whatever little resources we had. I was about to step onto the stage when, out of nowhere, Sukesh's sister, accompanied by her two siblings, appeared. She casually told us a sob story about her child being unwell. This couldn't possibly be true, as I saw that all three sisters were entirely made up. She didn't even apologise.

I was holding back my tears. I couldn't be seen on stage with teary eyes on such an important day. I went onto the stage without any makeup. How could she do this to me? She was blatantly lying. My tears continued to flow and showed no signs of stopping. I felt embarrassed to be on stage with eyes filled with tears.

Sukesh looked at me with concern and asked, "What's wrong?"

"Nothing," I managed a smile.

"Is something the matter? Are you not ready for this?" His face turned pale. I looked him in the eye, smiling and crying, a whirl of mixed emotions. Words wouldn't come out of my mouth, and I felt I would burst into tears. I was holding back. He was concerned now. He turned around and looked at my younger sister, signalling her to come near him. They spoke for a few seconds.

Sukesh turned towards me and said, "Hey, come on. That's alright. Someone as beautiful as you don't need makeup. I'll sponsor the best makeup artist for the wedding. Come on, get over it now, please. Smile."

Wow. That worked like magic. I knew he was flattering me, but it felt so good. I smiled, wiped away my tears, and stood there all the more determined and seemingly happy. Everything went well: the ritual of exchanging rings, the cake being cut, and guests arriving on stage to wish us and be photographed, followed by lunch and then the goodbyes.

This incident left a bitter taste in my mouth regarding how Sukesh's sisters had treated me. We had such a difficult existence, which is why I agreed to her offer of free makeup. It tears me up even now, thinking about it. Why did I need a beautician? I shouldn't have accepted her offer; I could have managed something by myself.

After the engagement, we returned home to reality. As usual, I was back to doing household chores; I did not have the luxury of daydreaming. Life in the village is not glamorous; it's very challenging. Everything needs to be done with clockwork precision. Since we were not there for the whole day, all the work that needed to be done had to be completed now. We all got busy with our activities and routines.

It was possibly a very enjoyable process for most of the girls, but the engagement brought more stress for me. I didn't look like a girl who had just got engaged a few hours earlier. I had a massive pile of dishes to wash as guests were home. Utensils were cleaned with wood ash; there was no fancy liquid soap—these were the dishwashing powders of village life. My mind was recalling all that had happened earlier. My hands were washing without active control when I suddenly heard a snap. I stopped in astonishment and wondered what had happened. My engagement ring had broken. I thought, what terrible quality of gold was this? I stared at my finger for quite some time. It did feel awful. Did it get damaged on the day of the engagement? I removed the ring and then put it back on again. I didn't want Amma to see it and get anxious. People at home might interpret it as a bad omen, perhaps.

The engagement took place in August, and the wedding date was set for December, a good five months later. After the engagement, Sukesh went back to Saudi Arabia. He returned to India in the last week of

November, after which he would call me daily. He had purchased smartphones for my younger sister and me.

Five months flew by in a blink. The day of the wedding was fast approaching. We were facing a shortfall of funds. There was a long list of expenses, even for the most basic necessities. I had asked Sukesh to purchase the *Karimani/Mangalsutra* as we couldn't afford it. My relatives contributed money and sarees, among other things. It is assumed that an Indian bride must be adorned in gold. Those who can afford it buy it. Often, people borrow from relatives. It would not do for me to return all the jewellery and be left with no gold. Therefore, we decided that at least one good gold chain had to be bought, and the rest borrowed from relatives.

I still remember when we went to purchase gold at the showroom; there was nothing we could buy with the cash we had. To say that our situation was pathetic would be an understatement. We settled on a long gold chain, but we were still short of some money. Then, my Amma removed the chain she was wearing and adjusted it to cover the remaining amount. I felt like crying. I asked myself; do I truly need to marry at this cost? There was still so much left to buy for the groom, and we could manage only one gold ring for him.

Mehendi

We had a pre-wedding ceremony known as the *"Madrangi/Mehendi"* [23], which was once again a very intimate occasion held individually at the bride and groom's homes. It is a simple ritual where Mehendi leaves are ground into a fine paste, and the bride's palms and fingertips are embellished with intricate designs. This ritual is typically performed after sunset.

Modern-day Mehendi ceremonies resemble a *Bollywood* [24] film in their grandeur, depending on the families' budgets. Hundreds of guests, lighting, DJ music, a special stage for the bride and groom, food, drinks, and themed attire—these were all distant dreams for me. With my aunts, cousins, sisters, and close friends combined, we had around 15 people at my Mehendi ceremony held at home.

Haldi

In this ritual, with close family members present, the bride and groom are given a bath in coconut milk mixed

---

23. Madrangi/Mehendi: The Mehendi leaves are ground and then the paste is applied on the hands and legs in various intricate designs which turn out reddish on the skin after the paste dries off.
24. Bollywood: Hindi-language Indian film industry

with turmeric at their respective homes. This is said to bestow a glow on the skin of the soon-to-be-weds. It is meant to be a very private affair. Who would want to bathe in public? However, in modern times, this has become a grand event in its own right. A special stage is set up, photographers and videographers are prepared, and the dress code is yellow, including the food. On the setup stage, turmeric-infused water is poured over the bride-to-be. Indeed, it's enjoyable for those who can afford it. I can't even recall if they performed this ritual for me.

Murthasese

It is an imperative ritual held at the bride's and groom's houses respectively a day before the wedding. In this ceremony, only the very close inner circle of the groom and the bride's relatives are invited to their respective homes. For some reason, this has remained a simple affair until now. My family members and I prayed to the sacred *Tulsi* [25] plant and were then seated on a chair facing east. My aunt initiated the ceremony by placing a toe ring on my second toe. The family members then

---

25. Tulsi: holy basil

came forward one by one and showered the sacred rice or the *Akshathe* [26] on my head as a form of blessing.

The Wedding

Indian weddings are a riot of colour, food, music, and festivities. Influenced by Bollywood films, South India has also adopted some North Indian customs, opulence, grandeur, and glamour. In our community, weddings were conducted at home. There was no priest involved; it was the elders from both sides who performed simple rituals. The most important is the "Kanyadaan" in Hindi or the "Daare" in my native Tulu language, followed by the tying of the Mangalsutra or Karimani [27] around the bride's neck. As people prospered, the number of rituals increased. Priests were introduced to conduct these rituals. Marriage ceremonies transitioned from the interwoven palm leaf-covered verandas of homes to air-conditioned marriage halls. Along with the weddings, lunches and dinners were also introduced.

On the wedding day, as we set off for the marriage hall, my Amma had only ₹4,000 in cash. How would we pay

---

26. Akshathe: Sacred rice usually dipped in red pigmented Kumkum and Turmeric
27. Mangalsutra/Karimani: a gold chain with black beads worn on the neck, symbolising a woman's marital status.

for the hall, bus, vehicles, and caterer? The wedding expenses fell entirely on us since there was no 'dowry' involved.

We reached the venue on time, and the sensation of having everyone's gaze upon me was exhilarating. When I opened the car door, the most pivotal figure in the Indian wedding scene was there to guide me: the photographer! From that moment on, he would choreograph every move I made—how I walked, smiled, posed, and even faked some of the smiles— literally everything. I stepped out of the car to the sound of trumpets at the entrance of this large white-coloured building. There stood my dear sisters-in-law to welcome me with the symbolic Arati [28]. I stepped through the beautifully decorated entrance of the marriage hall. My eyes drifted to the stage, which looked stunning with its floral decorations and ambient lighting. The ladies of the family escorted me onto the stage while a few children in their finest attire led the way. A red carpet covered the floor.

A few hundred guests were present, with some familiar faces scattered throughout. I managed to smile at them,

---

28. Arati: light (usually from a flame) is ritually waved for the veneration

though it felt awkward as all eyes seemed to be on me. I reached the stage first, followed by the groom entering the same entrance path.

With all the Hindu wedding rituals completed, people began queuing for the obligatory photograph with the bride and groom on stage. My cheeks and jaw ached from all the fake and genuine smiles I had to muster for the photographers. Lunch was over, the guests had departed, and my Amma and close relatives remained in the hall with a debt of ₹1 lakh. We requested a week from all the vendors to settle it and managed to pay it off by mortgaging my sister's gold chain. Finally, the wedding ceremony was concluded.

Back to Life in Tabuk

I had a three-month visa, and it had already been two and a half months since Saarika and I arrived in Tabuk, Saudi Arabia. Time flew by. Moosa, Sukesh's partner, was our visa sponsor. Consequently, Sukesh arranged for our visas to be renewed for another six months.

I used to call Amma daily and chat with her. For some strange reason, Amma still wasn't on speaking terms with Sukesh, which made things a bit awkward for me. However, Amma remained hesitant to believe that Sukesh had returned to his normal self. She kept cautioning me to be wary of his dealings. She asked me more questions about Sukesh than I ever asked him. I was unaware of any financial transactions involving Sukesh, as I didn't find it necessary to inquire, provided he supported my daughter and me.

I noticed that in recent days, Sukesh seemed rather dull. I didn't ask him why; he usually shared everything with me. I wondered what had happened and assumed he was missing his mother, to whom he was very attached. His mother felt the same way about him; she would feed him by hand whenever he returned home. He missed her while watching me have a video call with my mother and sisters. It had been almost two years since he last contacted his family. His family blamed me for keeping their son and brother away from them. I thought he might feel better if I encouraged Sukesh to speak to his parents.

One day, I sat beside him and said, "Why don't you call your father? I am a late addition to your life. Your father gave you your life and has cared for you since childhood. Even if he gets angry with you, that's fine. They may end up blaming me, and that's perfectly alright. Just listen to what they have to say. Speak to them without saying anything in my favour. Just call them and talk." He looked at me with longing eyes. I caressed his head, realising I had read his mind correctly. He mustered enough courage to call his father. As soon as the call connected, he began to cry and asked for forgiveness. His father was also crying on the other end, as I later learned through Sukesh. It seems he said, "You are my son after all. I won't let you go that easily." Sukesh also spoke to his mother. The conversation was quite lengthy and animated. I could overhear a few things but excused myself to the balcony. I didn't want him to feel awkward. However, I did turn around to see his face. It was a canvas of mixed emotions. They had a lot of catching up to do. I overheard him telling his parents not to blame me and that I was not the reason for his behaviour.

When the conversation finally drew close, I noticed his face turning a deep shade of red. He was immensely pleased to have spoken with them, which was a considerable relief. I also resolved to talk to them, bracing myself for any anger they might direct at me. At least the misunderstandings would be cleared up, and everyone would be content. Yet, I couldn't summon the courage to approach them. Sukesh began reaching out to his sisters as well. The phone calls between the family started occurring regularly, leading to a complete reconciliation.

Sukesh was kind to people. He was friendly with the Indian workforce diaspora, as he spoke Kannada and Hindi well. He also got on very well with the local Arabs, as he was fluent in Arabic, too. There were three *Kannada* [29] speaking men working for him. They were from a city called Belgaum in Karnataka. Moosa wasn't paying them their salaries properly. They even had their passports deposited with Moosa. Wanting to go home on holiday, they approached Sukesh for help. Sukesh

---

29. Kannada: Language spoken in the state of Karnataka, India

went to Moosa, retrieved the boys' passports, ensured they received their salaries and arranged for them to travel to India.

There was also an elderly man from Pakistan who was in his late sixties and had come to Saudi Arabia many years ago. Due to cataracts in his eyes, he struggled to see properly. He worked as a driver for a wealthy Arab who continually harassed him by refusing to grant him time off or to pay him his salary. Sukesh communicated with Moosa to contact the old man's employer and managed to secure the return of his passport. The employer, however, refused to pay his full dues and instead paid him some nominal amount. Eventually, Sukesh gave the old man some money and arranged for his return to Pakistan. He even bought clothes for the man's grandchildren, almonds, pistachios, dates, and chocolates. The old man began to cry profusely, expressing his deep gratitude to Sukesh. This was typical of him—going out of his way to help others.

One day, I asked him, "You help people so much. However, when we were in trouble, nobody assisted us. How is that justified?"

He replied, "That's fine. One day, you and our daughter will receive all that good karma back."

He was deeply concerned for others and was never jealous of anyone else's well-being. When his friends succeeded in life, he celebrated their achievements. Whenever we went to malls, he would give money to workers like sweepers, cleaners, janitors, and so on.

He recounted that he landed in Kuwait when he first arrived in the Middle East. The agent deceived him and got him to work on an oil rig. He wasn't paid, and he wasn't fed well. He stated, "These are the individuals who are often cheated. Many of them come from very poor financial backgrounds and arrive with a lot of dreams. They aim to earn in Riyals, which when converted to their local currencies back home—from wherever they have travelled, like India, Pakistan, or Bangladesh—results in a substantial amount that they could only dream of earning back home. They aspire to send money back home, support their families, marry off their sisters, educate their children, and help them escape poverty. This aspiration is driven by witnessing others in their town, locality, or village who have come to the Middle East and managed to build houses and improve their lifestyles back home."

These men were promised some employment. However, when they arrived, the agents took away their passports and placed them into hard, menial jobs unrelated to what they were initially promised. As a result, they found themselves trapped and, for their survival, began accepting any work offered to them. This is why he claimed to enjoy helping them.

Consequently, he garnered respect within the local Indian community. The local Arabs often view those of us from the subcontinent as inferior. However, Moosa, Sukesh's partner, who happened to be a local police officer, inexplicably held Sukesh in high regard, which Sukesh noted was rare. I witnessed this myself. One day, when Sukesh was ill, Moosa came looking for him. He forcibly took him to the hospital and ensured he received the necessary treatment. He also occasionally asked me to prepare Indian biriyani, which he adored. I had to reduce the spices somewhat, however. He seemed to be a genuinely kind man. Sukesh often remarked that he was a gem. While others mistreated those from the subcontinent, Moosa was different. He was very respectful and caring towards Sukesh.

The 15-day Desert Storm

We had our visas renewed in November. Around mid-December, I sensed something different about Sukesh's behaviour. He seemed very tense all the time. Was it his family again? Were they filling his head with new issues? However, he was speaking to his family, and I did not perceive any problems on that front. Saarika and he were the best of friends. I couldn't be happier, I suppose. What else was troubling him? My instincts were tingling. I hoped and prayed that he would not get into any trouble again. I tried asking him numerous times, but he avoided answering me and, with a straight face, left me perplexed.

I could not allow this situation to blow over. If anything, I needed to confront it now before it erupted in our faces. I cornered him one evening and asked,

"What is it?"

"What...?" he questioned back with a straight face.

"I've been observing that you've been under some stress for several days. Don't give me a nonsensical reason. I know there is something. Tell me. What is it?"

"……"

"I won't accept silence as an answer. You very well know I won't yield so easily. In this distant land, we only have each other to look out for one another. So, you'd better tell me."

"….."

I didn't give up. I sat directly in front of him, staring at his downcast face.

"Moosa…"

"Moosa and I started a new business in which he invested money. The business isn't performing well, and I cannot provide him with the kind of profit I promised. Now he is asking for his money back, and I cannot repay him."

"What business?"

"Real estate. We build small apartment complexes and sell the flats."

For some reason, I found that hard to believe. He didn't seem knowledgeable enough to construct buildings.

I said, "Come on. Don't feed me this story. I know it's something else."

"I promise, it's true. It's better you know only this much. The less you know, the better it is for you. So please don't ask me for more information."

I sat there, staring at him for a few moments, then got up and went to the bedroom. I was unsure but felt he wasn't telling me the whole truth. The less I knew, the better. What on earth is it now?

A couple of days passed, and it reached a point where he couldn't sleep at all. When asked, he would say, "I can't sleep due to the stress." He also experienced nightmares. He would wake up screaming, "They're going to kill me." I would then switch on the TV and join him in watching a show.

He had another good friend, Latif, who lived in Dammam, on the eastern end of Saudi Arabia, while we were situated on the western end. They spoke to each other daily over the phone in Arabic. Sukesh would occasionally mention that Latif was a good friend of his. That was all I knew about Latif.

One day, he said, "I'll go to Dammam. Latif owes me money. I'll get the money and give it to Moosa." For some reason, I sensed that he wasn't sharing the full extent of the problem. I didn't want to pry either. A phrase stuck in my mind: 'The less you know, the better it is.' I didn't make any effort to inquire further. There wasn't much I could do anyway. It was his problem; he would solve it. Everything around me felt so dreamlike that I didn't want to disrupt it.

Day 01

On the morning of December 21st, he departed for Dammam, saying, "If you two need anything, tell Aslam. He'll get it for you." Aslam was a lad working in his shop, and I had his number. He also added, "Keep yourself locked inside. I'll go to Dammam and set things right."

Lock ourselves inside? There goes my spider sense again... I feared something was amiss but didn't want to believe it. I prayed, hoping my instincts were wrong. Just when life was settling down, I didn't want to jeopardise that.

He took the early morning flight. Saarika had woken as soon as Sukesh did; such was her attachment to him. Saarika and I went to the airport to see him off. He approached the gate, turned around, returned, and said, "If you have any ill feelings towards me, please don't take them out on our daughter." There he goes again with his cryptic talk.

After reaching Dammam, he called me to say he had arrived. The air conditioning in the house wasn't working, so I told him it needed to be repaired. He mentioned he would ask Aslam to fix it and that his friend in Dammam, Latif, was on duty. He would collect the cheque from him as soon as Latif returned and then head back to Tabuk. I noticed there was a call waiting; it was Sukesh's father. Sukesh's father stayed in regular touch with both me and Sukesh. He would likely have tried to call Sukesh, but upon finding his mobile busy, he must have called me instead.

I received his call after finishing with Sukesh. He asked me where Sukesh was, and I informed him that Sukesh had gone to Dammam. I could sense a tone of alarm in his voice. For some reason, he never totally believed his son. He asked me if Latif truly owed him money and whether Sukesh would return. He started to cry, asking if I knew what was going on. He inquired, "Has this fellow started his financial irregularities again?"

I was jolted. I said, "Nothing like that, *Mama* [30]. He has gone to Latif's place. I'm sure it's nothing to worry about. Yes, he has been tense for a few days, but I don't

---

30. Mama: In this context, father-in-law is referred to as "Mama" in Tulu language.

think there is any need for concern. You relax. I'll ask him to call you when he's back home." And I ended the call. But my mind was racing. I could feel my head heating up, and I started to sweat. I just consoled myself that nothing was wrong. He would return by evening, and things would be back to how they were.

Day 02

I called him first thing in the morning and asked whether everything was done. Had he settled the finances? He sounded very relaxed and said, "Yes, everything is done. I will come back in the evening." I was completely tense, but after hearing his tone, it felt somewhat comforting. I was living alone with a one-and-a-half-year-old baby in this foreign land. I wondered why his father became so tense when I told him about his visit to Dammam. Am I missing something here? Are there more skeletons in the cupboard? I was growing restless.

I made a video call to Sukesh last night, but he didn't answer. Fifteen minutes later, I made a voice call, and this time, he responded. I asked him, "Why didn't you answer the video call? Saarika wanted to speak to you. She's missing you." I was trying to gauge his mood; he seemed normal. He spoke to Saarika and mentioned that he was still caught up in the negotiation and wouldn't be able to leave tonight. He said he would come the following day. I found it hard to make sense of anything as doubts crept into my mind. Was he telling me the truth? Was there something more going on? Would he come back at all? Why did his father say that?

Day 03

I called him again in the morning. I couldn't sleep well at night. He answered the call and said, "I've landed myself in a bad situation. I can't do anything. I think I'm going to die. I'm unable to arrange the funds. Moosa is calling me continuously. I was annoyed with him for calling me so many times. In a fit of anger, I told him to get lost and that I wasn't going to give his money back. Let him do what he can. I don't want to cheat him, but my situation is what it is." I was utterly dumbfounded hearing this. I went emotionless momentarily, just trying to grasp what he was telling me.

"Knock… Knock…" Someone was knocking at the door. I informed Sukesh that someone was at the door.

Sukesh raised his voice and almost shouted, "It must be Moosa. Just tell him everything will be alright. That I'll settle his money."

While Sukesh was on the phone, I walked to the door and opened it. There stood, as rightly guessed by Sukesh, Moosa and Aslam. I asked Aslam what the matter was. Aslam replied, "Moosa *saab* [31] says your husband's phone is switched off. He owes money to Moosa Saab and has also informed him that he will go to Dammam to retrieve the money. However, he hasn't returned yet." He paused, glanced back at Moosa, and then turned towards me. "And he also abused Moosa saab over the phone."

I said, "That's not possible. His phone isn't switched off; he's on the line right now. I've been talking to him this whole time. Here, talk to him." I passed the phone to Aslam when I realised the call had been disconnected. I redialled Sukesh's number, and to my surprise, I received a message indicating that the phone was switched off on the other end.

I was perplexed. Moosa had been standing behind Aslam all this time. He was a medium-built man with a trimmed beard, dressed in his *Abaya* [32]. Soft-spoken and well-mannered, he treated Sukesh and me respectfully during our limited interactions. Until now,

---

31. Saab: An honorary to someone superior in position.
32. Abaya: a piece of loose over-garment worn in the Arab world

Moosa had been looking away, but he turned to me and said, "He won't come back ever, sister. He owes me money. He will abscond from Dammam." Aslam translated his words softly.

I said, "That's not possible, Moosa *bhai*. How can he abscond, leaving his wife and child? Where will he go? He should be coming back." My voice was trembling by now.

Moosa looked at me with a long pause and said, "No, sister, he's not the kind of person you think he is. He won't come back ever. Some of our friends got together and invested in him. He's mismanaged the finances and now is unable to return the money to us. He had promised to pay back the first instalment of money today. But it seems like he won't be able to arrange such a large amount. He has to take out a loan again to repay us. Who will lend him money? We've been with him for so many years, so we believed in him and invested. He betrayed our trust. He has put me in serious trouble." I could see the dejected look on Moosa's face, but I didn't have the nerve to ask him for details. I didn't want to involve myself more than I currently knew of.

All three of us stood near the door for some time without a word spoken, which felt like an hour. Then Moosa said, "Sister, it is not safe for you to stay here alone with the kid. You better come to my house." I couldn't understand what he was trying to say. I said, "I can't do that, Moosa bhai. I'm not going anywhere, come what may." My usual defence mechanism took over. I had been in worse situations but never got bogged down by anything or anyone. The only difference here was that I was in a foreign country with a kid.

Alarm bells were ringing all over me. Moosa was looking at a distance, lost in thought. And then he just walked off. Aslam looked at me helplessly and walked behind him. It was like he was trying to tell me, "I'm helpless. I'm just a translator here."

After they left, I tried to analyse the situation. The questions crashed in like waves: "What's happening? Why did Moosa ask me to go with him? Will he keep me as one of his wives? I've heard stories that they keep slave wives here. They can have multiple wives under the law. Will he convert me to Islam? Will I ever be able to go back home? See Amma and my sisters? Oh, God."

Why did Moosa say it's not safe here? Was it for my own good he was saying so? Did he mean that his other partners might harm me? From what I know of Moosa, he was a very good human. Or perhaps they would keep me as their wife? I was sweating profusely. I told myself to remain calm. Let me tackle one challenge at a time. Sukesh's phone was switched off the entire day. I didn't know what to do. I didn't have Latif's number. By nightfall, I was utterly exhausted. I was plagued by nightmares that someone was knocking at the door.

Day 04

I was serving breakfast to Saarika in the morning when, yet again, there was a knock at the door. I prayed to God it would be Sukesh. I would beg him to send me and Saarika back to India, letting him deal with all this madness alone. I opened the door and saw a lady in a burqa, along with Moosa and Aslam. Aslam said, "Bhabhi, you'd best come with them to their house. There are a lot of complications. It's not safe for you to stay here. Sukesh won't return; he owes them nearly 1 crore in Indian money."

I was on the verge of breaking down, tears streaming down my face. I stood there, crying, while Aslam tried to comfort me, saying it was the best course of action to take now.

I invited them inside. Moosa's wife attempted to console me, with Aslam translating her words. She kept insisting that it was unsafe for me to live alone here. They were pressuring me to go to their house. I wasn't certain whether they were friends or foes. Were they genuinely concerned for my well-being, or were they holding me and Saarika as pawns to extract Sukesh from his hideout? I felt like calling Amma, but my mobile phone credit had run out. I had updated her on everything going on here, and I was relieved knowing she had the correct information about me and Saarika. I repeatedly asked them why I couldn't stay in this house and why it wasn't safe for us to live there, but they did not answer my question.

Eventually, I had to relent to their demands. They were persistent, and there wasn't much I could do. I didn't have enough money to sustain myself if Sukesh didn't return within a week. I packed some clothes for Saarika and me. I wasn't sure how much to carry or how many days I would be staying at their house. I dreaded asking them that question. I was ready with my bag. I got into Moosa bhai's big car. He drove with his wife, sitting beside me at the back and Aslam in the front passenger seat.

After ten minutes of driving, we arrived at this large bungalow. Holding Saarika on my hip, I got down and dragged my bag along. As soon as we entered the living room, Moosa's wife asked me to sit on the sofa and said something in Arabic. Three children were running around in the living area. The floor was carpeted, and some large portraits hung on the walls. There were crossed swords and an antique rifle. The ceiling was dome-shaped and quite high—perhaps 15 feet.

I was observing the ceiling dome when I heard someone speaking in Arabic. It was Moosa's wife, who was wearing loose floral trousers and a full-sleeved shirt, along with a dark blue hijab that complemented her milky white complexion. She was beautiful and held two glasses of cold juice in her hands. I thanked her for the drinks as Saarika, and I sipped on them.

She asked me to remove my burqa and hang it on the wooden pole in the corner. I could see two more children; they were toddlers. The last one was just beginning to walk, possibly. There were five children, and I assumed they all belonged to her. They must be roughly a year apart, with the eldest around five to six years old. Saarika reluctantly tried to make friends with them, as she was not accustomed to being around other children her age.

Saarika and I were confined to the living room. I didn't have access to any rooms apart from the living room, an attached washroom, and the kitchen. The space featured a lovely carpet and air conditioning, keeping it cool. A television was present, and Saarika watched it with the children. I made myself comfortable, watching TV with them at the edge of the sofa, but my mind was elsewhere. Thousands of questions about Sukesh, my fate, and my child's future filled my thoughts.

It was afternoon when Moosa's wife arrived with a large plate filled with rice and meat. It consisted of rice and a whole chicken cooked with spices. Everyone had to eat from the same large plate: Moosa's wife, their five children, my daughter, and I. This was a culture shock for both Saarika and me. Everyone gathered around the plate on the dining table, and Moosa's wife gestured for me to eat. I was unsure what to do, as we were not accustomed to this practice. Eating from the same plate? Couldn't we have our own plates to serve food from the larger one? I signalled her for a plate, but she either didn't grasp my request or chose to ignore it and began eating. They all started sharing from the same large plate.

I was hungry, and so was Saarika. I scooped some rice and chicken meat with my hands and took my first mouthful. There were no onions, garlic, tomatoes, or spices—nothing. It was just bland. But I had to eat. I urged Saarika to eat, but she was unwilling.

This was the situation each time. Some children had runny noses and were eating with the same hand. It was repulsive to me. Moosa's wife insisted that I eat. I found it incredibly difficult to do so. The food had no seasoning, and I felt like crying whenever I had to eat it. Two days passed, and Saarika would ask for biscuits, chocolates, etc. Where would I obtain them for her? Moosa brought her chips once. Whenever she was hungry, I fed her my already-weaning breast milk. I was so hungry, too. I often wondered if only they would allow me to make Tomato Rasam [33] I would have cooked it myself and eaten it with plain rice. Later, Saarika became so accustomed to their rice and chicken that she would call me whenever food was served. Surprisingly, she had previously disliked rice. Due to my hunger pangs, I, too, had to adapt and eat whatever was offered.

Moosa's wife was so engrossed in her work that she didn't have time to look after their children. There were already five of them; the youngest was less than a year old. That child

33. Rasam: A watery soup filled with spices, made in south India.

was often neglected when it cried. She would walk around as if nothing was happening. The most she would do was pour orange juice into the feeding bottle and hand it to the infant. Later, that child would look up to me to be held and cared for, and I could not resist the motherly instinct to soothe the child. She wouldn't even bother to change the diapers. Once, it so happened that she and Moosa had gone out to a wedding, leaving the youngest one with me. I noticed the diaper needed changing, and when I removed it, to my horror, the area was covered in rashes. I then bathed her and found a first aid kit in the kitchen. I applied ointment to the rashes. I had never seen Moosa's wife bathe the children nor even brush their teeth. The mother even used to hit the children with flip-flops if they misbehaved.

Day 05

Day 06

Day 07

Day 08

Day 09

Life was becoming monotonous. I didn't know how many more days this would continue. I stopped overthinking. I stopped thinking altogether. I felt like a zombie. I would wake up, eat, sleep, and watch TV. That's all I did. I stopped thinking about Sukesh as well. I was hoping for a miracle—that Sukesh would reappear just as he had the last time in Mumbai. I desperately wanted to call my Amma. I knew she would be extremely worried. They had taken away my mobile phone. I asked them to give me my mobile so I could call my family back home in India, but Moosa's wife refused.

Due to the language barrier, I couldn't communicate with Moosa's wife. She could only understand Arabic. Whatever little conversation we had was usually conducted through sign language. I spoke to her in English, and she replied in Arabic. I was so frustrated that I occasionally used profanities during our discussions.

Day 10

The day began like any other, with me lost in my thoughts as I sat by the living room window. Suddenly, I heard footsteps behind me and turned to see Moosa and his wife approaching. Instinctively, I pulled my dupatta over my head—a reflex born from the deep-rooted influence of the culture surrounding me. Moosa's wife extended her hand to give me my mobile. I wondered why there was this sudden change of heart. I looked both of them in the eye and slowly extended my hand to take the mobile from her.

Moosa asked me to call Sukesh. Although I did not understand Arabic, he spoke in broken English and Arabic. Moosa stood beside me and requested that I put it on speaker. I called Sukesh, and he answered. As soon as he spoke from the other side, Moosa snatched the phone from me. When Sukesh heard Moosa's voice, he disconnected. Moosa began shouting in frustration. Although I did not comprehend a word he said, the emotion behind the words was obvious. Moosa hurried out of the living room with my phone.

Later that evening, Moosa returned and asked me to call again. It was the same: Sukesh would answer and then disconnect as soon as Moosa spoke. Moosa was furious once more.

Day 11

In the evening, I was combing Saarika's hair. I gave her a head bath today. At home, I would apply oil and plait it into small braids, even though she did not have long hair. But she loved braids. Through the window, I saw Aslam walking past. For no reason, my heartbeat began to quicken. Had he come for me or to speak to Moosa's wife? He had indeed come for me.

"Bhabhi, they have found Sukesh."

"———"

"Moosa bhai has asked you to come."

"Oh God. My prayers have been answered. Trouble in India, and when I prayed, we came to Saudi Arabia. Trouble in Saudi Arabia. Where else should I be going? Why is this man a magnet for trouble?"

I walked towards my burqa and wore it hurriedly. I accompanied him, carrying Saarika on my waist. My eyes widened. He led me to a large room attached to the main house but accessible from the outside. We exited the house and entered this large room again through a different door.

As soon as I entered, I noticed four more people besides Moosa. I was taken aback to see Sukesh seated in one corner with his head bowed. I slowly approached him, placed my hand gently on his shoulder, and nearly whispered in our mother tongue, Tulu, *"Volu ittarye eeth dina?* (Where have you been all these days?)" I could see some streaks of blood on his hand. I wondered if I was dreaming. I hoped not.

Aslam asked me to speak in Kannada since he was from Belgaum and could speak and understand Kannada but not Tulu. He was tasked to translate what Sukesh and I discussed to Moosa and his friends. I refused to speak in Kannada, as I didn't care if they understood or not. It was far more important for me to talk to Sukesh and learn the truth. Then, the men began shouting at me to speak in Kannada. I was frightened and started to cry. I began asking him in Kannada.

At that time, he confessed, "I took money from them and am unable to repay. You and Saarika need to find a way to return to India. They won't let me go." I asked him what the lines on his hand were. He replied, "They hit me with wires." My stomach churned. I noticed he had ink on his thumb. I said, "What's that?" pointing at his thumb. He said, "They have no proof of paying me, so they've taken my thumb impression on the paper." He still refused to raise his head, not looking at me or his daughter. Saarika was frightened as the people shouted. She remained silent, staring at her father.

My heart melted at the sight of his condition. He had always been smartly dressed, but now he looked shabby. He wore the same shirt and trousers he had on the day he left for Dammam. All my anger towards him for putting us in this situation vanished, and I was overwhelmed with sympathy for him. He must have endured physical torment. I could only see injuries on his hands; God knows where else he has been harmed.

He turned to Saarika and extended his hands. She was scared and did not approach him, prompting Moosa to say something. I asked Aslam to translate for me. "They're saying even his daughter knows what a rascal he is. Even she doesn't want to be near him."

I stood there, fixating my gaze on Sukesh. Tears streamed down my face. Sukesh sat with his arms folded across his chest, staring at the floor. I didn't know whether to pity this husband of mine, to lament my fate, to feel sorry for my daughter for having been born to us, or to sympathise with my mother for enduring this through no fault of her own.

I was then asked to leave. As I walked back, I felt utterly helpless and furious. I didn't know what to do; I felt like I couldn't do anything. What a mess I was trapped in.

I had no idea how they managed to catch hold of him. I would guess that they blackmailed him using me and our daughter as leverage. Or perhaps they tracked his cell tower and calls. Moosa was a local policeman. He might have used his contacts to locate him in Dammam. My mobile was returned to me after they apprehended him. I called Amma to update her on the situation. Amma was relieved to hear my voice, yet distraught at the same time. Her fears about Sukesh getting into trouble were proven correct. She asked me when we were moving back to India. Honestly, I did not have an answer to that. I was unsure about what further drama awaited me and my daughter—or my husband for that matter. I had resolved that whatever it was, I would confront it. That was the only way to deal with this.

Day 12

I couldn't sleep the entire night. As soon as I woke up, I wondered where they must have kept him. I couldn't see him online anywhere on WhatsApp or Facebook. Meanwhile, Moosa's wife began to question me. Since she couldn't communicate verbally, she used Google Translate. She asked if we had any property in India and whether I had gold jewellery. I replied that I had no idea about Sukesh's financial dealings with them and that I didn't have any property or jewellery. My only answer was "I DO NOT KNOW". She forced me to accompany her to a ladies-only park nearby in the evening. I was in no mood to go anywhere. But still, she insisted. I was wondering why she was forcing me to come. It did not occur to me that they had kept Sukesh locked up in the house. Maybe they were interrogating him, torturing him, and possibly they didn't want me to hear his screams.

Later that evening, I noticed that Sukesh was online on WhatsApp and Facebook. A small glimmer of hope emerged. I messaged him, aware that whoever was surrounding him might be peering at his mobile. However, he never replied to my messages. I sent him numerous messages, desperately writing, "How could you do this to me? How could you do this to your daughter? Why do we deserve this punishment?" I poured out my frustrations in lengthy messages.

Later, I discovered that he was online because he was calling India. He contacted his father and his sisters, asking for money. They made him do that, but nobody responded positively. How could they? Why would they? Deep down, he knew that as well. However, he might have called due to pressure from Moosa and his friends.

Day 13

I returned from the bathroom after brushing my teeth. I checked my mobile and found Sukesh's voice message on WhatsApp.

> *"I have been involved in some financial misdealing. I own some property in Dammam. I will sell it and repay all the creditors. Please forgive me. I realise I've caused you difficulty. It's merely a matter of time. I will come through this. Then we'll return to India and settle down there."*

I replied, "I cannot forgive you any longer. I cannot believe you any longer. I have had enough of you. I want to take my child back to India. I have nothing to do with you anymore. I'm fed up with your antics."

Surprisingly, he replied immediately, "Please don't say that. They're not giving me water to drink, either. They're going to kill me. Even if I survive, I'm not in a position to return to India. I can't show my face to anyone any longer." I had had enough of him. Enough of all this drama. I just wanted to take Saarika back to my village. I'll earn a living somehow back home. It's safer and more beautiful back home than this foreign land. I don't need a husband anymore. I'm exhausted. Exhausted!

Abdul Rehman Alias Sukesh Shetty:

I knew that they used to call him Abdul Rehman. He would tell me that he believed in Islam. He even confided in me that he wanted to undertake the holy pilgrimage to Mecca. I thought he must have changed his belief system. I never imagined he had converted to Islam. Even then, I could do nothing as I was already married to him. He was a Muslim in Saudi Arabia and a Hindu in India. During Ramadan, he fasted like any devout Muslim. I had no problem with that as long as he cared for my daughter and me. Occasionally, he would ask me to convert to Islam and undertake Namaz. But I stood my ground and said, "I respect your decision and belief, so you respect mine. Please don't force me." he never did after that. During Ramadan, when they broke the fast in the evening, I would cook for all of them: he and the boys from the workshop.

Aslam:

He was a nice boy who used to call me Bhabhi [34]He hailed from Belgaum, from the state of Karnataka in India. Sukesh occasionally took some food that I cooked for the boys. He was a very strict taskmaster. He would shout at the boys often if they made any mistakes. I felt he was rude at times. I wonder if Aslam held some grudge against Sukesh. Nevertheless, he was a nice boy as far as I knew him; he was always kind to me and treated me with respect.

Moosa:

He was either a police officer or an inspector; I'm not certain. Both he and his wife were reasonably good to me. Whenever I cried, Moosa comforted me by saying, "You are my sister; I won't harm you," and so on. I still hold him in high regard. Once, when Sukesh fell ill, Moosa visited our flat to check on him. Sukesh noted that local Saudis typically do not care for immigrants. Even Sukesh

---

34. Bhabhi: sister-in-law in Hindi

acknowledged that Moosa was a genuinely nice chap. Nobody else does what he does. Whenever Moosa came home, he would ask for Indian chai (with milk). Sukesh admired him, often saying Moosa looked after him like a brother. This made me ponder: if the Saudi man was so good to him, Sukesh must have done something terrible to shake his faith in him, leading to his change of heart.

My domain was the living area, which was quite spacious. A television displayed cartoons on a continuous loop. There was an attached washroom for our use. I never ventured out of this area for the entire time I was there. I did not know where Sukesh was; he must have been kept in another part of the house.

Though the thought crossed my mind, escaping from the house was never an option. Escape to where? I didn't know the language, I didn't know the place, and I didn't have money or my passport; where would I take my daughter along? They were feeding both me and my daughter well. There was no imminent danger that I could foresee. Deep down, I somehow knew that one day or another, Sukesh, a clever bloke, would work something out and take us back to India. He would be released sooner or later. To contact anyone, I had to rely on an internet connection. There was no currency on my phone. I used to send voice messages to my Amma via WhatsApp, connected via Moosa's wi-fi network. This was my routine.

Day 14

I was tired in the evening as I had woken up early that day. As usual, I used to have very disturbed sleep daily. I would sleep on the carpet with Saarika by my side. They had provided me with pillows and bed sheets. Saarika had already fallen asleep. I was setting my pillow to sleep when Moosa's wife entered. She typed something into Google Translate. It said, "Sukesh has returned 40 Lakhs. He owes us another 50 Lakhs. You decide what you want to do. Do you want to stay and work here, or do you want to go back to India? You can go back, but we will not allow him to leave. He has to pay all our money, and only then shall we allow him to go." I was in a state of confusion. 40 Lakh? What? Indian Rupees or Riyals? Where did he arrange that kind of money from? Has this lady mistakenly typed an extra zero? I was so confused. There was no chance he would have that much money to give them. But whatever it was, wherever he had arranged it from, I was happy that our ordeal was ending. I shall seek all answers from Sukesh himself once we are through this.

I sighed in relief. I sent a voice message to Amma explaining all the details. I said, "I will come back to India soon." I went off to sleep. I used to keep my mobile next to my head while sleeping. That was my only important link to the outside world—the sole communication medium with my family.

Day 15

I woke up relatively late that morning. Perhaps I had managed to get a good night's sleep. My usual morning routine involved checking my phone for a voice message from my family or sending them one myself. However, I couldn't find my mobile. I began searching for it. There was no way I could have misplaced it, as no one had entered the hall after I went to sleep. I searched for a while and then realised it wasn't there. They must have taken it. But why?

I had never ventured into their house beyond the living room and the adjoining kitchen. I thought that Moosa's wife might know something. I set off to find her and ask if she knew where my mobile was. I made my way into the inner part of the house, which I had never seen or dared to enter. Four ladies were seated in one of the rooms with Moosa's wife. She was crying uncontrollably while the others comforted her. I walked in and asked,

"What happened?" She didn't respond. I asked her, "Where is my mobile?" I was not concerned about why she was crying; I just wanted my mobile at any cost. She continued to cry. Eventually, I moved away from the room. There was a door leading out of the house next to it, and as I passed by, I saw a crowd of people in the open lawn area. It appeared that some police officers were present as well. As soon as they saw me, everyone began to stare. I wondered why. What was wrong? Was I dreaming? I tried to open my eyes wide. Nothing. I wasn't dreaming.

A man approached me. He came closer and spoke in Hindi, asking me to wear the Burqa. Nothing made sense.

I went inside to put on the burqa. By that time, my daughter had also woken up from her sleep. I quickly went to the washroom with Saarika, freshened up, donned the burqa, and returned to the courtyard. The man speaking in Hindi asked me, "What is Abdul Rehman to you?

"My husband."

"Where is he now?"

"I don't know."

"What do you mean you don't know?"

I replied, "It's been 15 days since I last saw him. The house owner, Moosa, would know where he is. There was a bit of a disagreement between my husband and Moosa, so only he knows where he is. I have no idea."

I saw that the police officer standing there had both Sukesh's and my mobile phone in his hand. I wondered why he had Sukesh's mobile. My mind was trying to make sense of the situation. There was a small outhouse attached to the bungalow. Usually, they would bring male guests and have a party, if at all. The officers were standing outside that room. My worst fear was that Sukesh must have had an altercation and hit Moosa during the incident. I thought Sukesh must be in jail and Moosa in the hospital. That was why his wife was crying so much. My imagination was working overtime now.

I asked the man who spoke to me in Hindi what had happened. One of the officers there told him to inform me to pack my luggage. I asked him, "Why? Why do I need to go with them? What has happened?" He was not saying anything to me. I was so frightened. I was palpitating. I didn't know what to do. There was nobody I knew around. Not even Aslam.

Did I have to go with the police? What would they do? Where would my child and I be? How would they treat us? I couldn't make sense of what was happening. I had no choice; I had to go. I went inside, packed my small cabin bag and a backpack, and placed all my faith in God as I started. I knew I hadn't done anything wrong. God would take care of me. Mankind's last refuge when no one is around... God!

Alongside my daughter, I sat in the police vehicle with my travel bag. I didn't know where they were taking us. I couldn't understand a word of the Arabic they were speaking. After about a 15-minute drive, they stopped outside a medium-sized white building. The officers asked me to sit in a room attached to the main building. A lady was sitting there, and they requested that I sit with her. I didn't know who she was; her face was covered with a burqa. After about 30 minutes, another lady came in wearing a burqa. I didn't know her either. She was crying incessantly. I could tell that she was Moosa's wife. She sat 20 feet away from me.

After some time, she was called, and she left the premises. The lady sitting next to me asked me to lie down and take a nap. I declined, as I wasn't sleepy. I wanted a mobile phone now; I needed to call my Amma to update her on what was happening. I didn't know where I was. It looked like a hospital. I didn't know who was hospitalised. Was Sukesh hospitalised? Then why was Moosa's wife crying? That cannot be the case. I think Moosa has been hospitalised. Sukesh must have hit him or something. Oh God, how much more do I have to endure?

After about an hour, I noticed a family walking past. They were undoubtedly Indians or perhaps Pakistanis, speaking in Hindi. I mustered my courage and approached them. I began chatting in the broken Hindi I could manage. They asked me, "What is the matter? Why are you here?" I replied, "My husband must have done something; I have no idea what it is." I asked the lady if she could lend me her mobile phone, as I needed to call my Amma in India. She was generous enough to let me use her phone. I called Amma and informed her of all that had transpired since morning, mentioning that I was at the police station. I said either Moosa or Sukesh had been arrested and would let her know as soon as I found out, provided they returned my phone. I asked her not to try to reach me since I didn't have my phone. I couldn't afford to speak for long as I was on a borrowed phone. I urged Amma to stay strong, which she was. I sincerely thanked the lady and returned her mobile. The reason I told Amma I was at the police station was that I could see some people inside wearing uniforms, so I was sure this was a police station. I wondered how my mother would take this news; I couldn't imagine. I knew she was a remarkably strong lady, but no matter how strong she was, I understood this news would unsettle her.

The family that assisted me appeared to know what had transpired. It was a relatively small place. They had come to the station to complain about the fire in their shop. They must have heard about this incident. Crime is rare in this country due to the severity of punishments. Any such news would spread like wildfire. They genuinely cared for me, and the lady handed over 100 Riyals. I refused, stating I didn't need it, but they insisted I take it. I wondered how they were aware of my situation. What prompted them to show such kindness towards me? They also said, "Allah will take care. Don't worry." Nothing made sense to me; I could only speculate. I was left wondering whether Sukesh was the perpetrator or the victim. If he was the victim, had he been seriously injured? My mind was racing.

After a while, the police brought my daughter some biscuits, juice, and crisps. I wondered why. Did it mean that they wouldn't let me go? Would they lock me up? Time seemed to drag on. I was struggling to understand what was real. I still hadn't been informed about what was happening. I didn't have a phone to speak to my people back in India. At least that would have lightened my heart.

Then, a police officer arrived. He handed me a phone. Someone was speaking in Hindi on the other end. He began asking questions. The reception was very poor. I couldn't properly hear what he was saying, nor could he understand me.

The Reveal

It was 11:30 at night. Saarika was fast asleep. I was bored, anxious, hungry, and feeling nauseous all at once. Aside from a lady in a burqa sitting next to me, there was nobody else in the large, well-lit hall.

The lady in the burqa next to me walked inside. She came out and gestured for me to go in. I was about to pick up Saarika, who was sleeping on the bench, when the lady in the burqa motioned for me to let her sleep, assuring me that she would keep an eye on her. All in sign language. I stepped into a neatly arranged small office. Two people were seated there: one was a police officer, and the other was dressed in a thawb, the traditional Arabic dress. He spoke Hindi. They asked me to sit down, and the Arabic man began questioning me in heavily accented Hindi. The police officer seemed to be taking down my statement. I had to recount everything. When had I last seen Sukesh? How many of them were there at that time? What had I observed? About the physical injuries, the mood of the individuals, Sukesh's mental and physical condition, whether there had been a dispute with Sukesh, and what that dispute was about, etc. I conveyed everything I was aware of.

I said, "I haven't seen my husband for the last 10 days." Then they asked me, "Do you wish to see your husband?" It was then that I realised they had arrested him. I began to cry. I said, "I don't want to see him. He has misled me everywhere. I want to return to India with my daughter. I don't want to see him. Please send me back to India."

The person speaking in Hindi insisted. He asked, "Don't you want to see him at least once for the last time?" I began sobbing uncontrollably. I replied, "Alright, let me see him once." Both of them exchanged glances.

He continued, "God has willed everyone their destiny. Your husband is no more!"

I abruptly stopped sobbing and was unable to comprehend what he had just said. I sat there, dumbstruck. This was beyond doubt regarding what must have occurred. Dead? I was in utter shock. I uttered, "What?" That's what I remember last.

When I regained consciousness, the lady in the burqa was holding me, sprinkling water on my face. I began crying again. They all attempted to console me. The man speaking Hindi said, "Look at your child, and for the kid's sake, you must be strong." I fell silent after a while. My tears dried up. Saarika was asleep on the bench we were sitting on.

The two police officers and the woman in a burqa were seated on chairs in front of me. I asked the police, "How did he die?" The officer said, "As you stated in your account, they have beaten him, tortured him, and possibly due to that, he died." I felt even more aggrieved. The churn in my stomach wouldn't cease. Oh God, did they really have to kill him? And by torturing him too?

An Angel in the Desert of Uncertainty

I spent the night reminiscing about my life. It was now 8 a.m. The Arab translator approached me and asked if I had any friends or relatives there. I replied no. He mentioned that I would be taken to a hostel for ladies, where my daughter and I would be accommodated for a while until the investigation was concluded. After that, arrangements would be made for our return to India.

I asked, "Why can't I go back to the house I lived in?" The translator replied that this would not be possible at the time.

I said I wanted to go to our house to collect mine and my child's clothes. They asked me for the address. I replied that I didn't know but was certain my house was near Moosa's place.

Saarika had woken up by now and was quite fussy. All she did was eat the biscuits and crisps that the police had offered. I also satisfied my hunger with that.

After thirty minutes, he returned and asked us to follow him. He led us to the police SUV, which took us to our flat. Fortunately, I had the keys with me. As soon as I entered, the familiar smell of 'home' welcomed me after so many days. I wished they would allow me to stay there. I began packing what I needed. My daughter picked up a few toys for herself. I opened Sukesh's wardrobe and randomly picked out a few of his shirts. I just did it instinctively. I held one of his shirts close to my face and could smell him. Sukesh had this peculiar body odour. I burst into tears again. I couldn't believe he was no longer alive. The officers were urging me gently to hurry up. I sobbed throughout. I took a last glance around. I knew it would be my final time in this house. It was such a lovely, short-lived dream. We had plans—plans for the long term. I stepped outside and locked the door. When the officer asked me to hand over the keys, I hesitated. He told me I would receive an acknowledgement, as the landowner needed to be informed.

We got back into the SUV once more. The translator handed my mobile phone back to me. I tried calling Amma, but her number was unreachable. I then called my brother-in-law. I needed to make use of whatever little time I had before they possibly snatched my phone away again. I briefly recounted the story to him. He was shocked to hear that Sukesh was no more. He tried comforting me, saying, "You are just like my sister; I shall take care of things for you. Don't worry, I shall work something out." I attempted to call Amma again, but the battery had already drained, and my phone switched off. I was relieved that I could at least inform my brother-in-law. They drove us to a location twenty minutes away. The lady in the Burqa was also sitting with me in the back of the SUV. We arrived at a mid-sized building. I had no idea where we were. The lady accompanying me began shouting at her male counterparts. Only then did I realise she was a police officer. We got out of the SUV and walked inside the building. Another lady wearing a Hijab was seated there. The two conversed in Arabic and exchanged some paperwork. Finally, the lady cop hugged me and left.

We had reached a hostel. A women's hostel. There was a reception counter, and the receptionist asked me to remove all the gold and my mobile phone that I was carrying. She requested that I keep them in the safe deposit there. I couldn't understand her language, and she couldn't understand mine, but she communicated with me in sign language. I wanted my mobile but couldn't argue; I just had to listen to whatever they said. Then, a lady came along to help my daughter and me carry our luggage. They allocated a room for me. It was a plain-looking building, similar to any college hostel, with ground plus two floors. There was a translucent, roofing-covered veranda in the middle and rooms arranged circularly all around. My small room had a double bunk bed, air-conditioning, a long mirror, and a wardrobe, perhaps meant for two people. My room was empty. There were common bathrooms lined up in one corner of the floor. After a tiring night, we settled down.

I woke up early and stepped out of the room to find that a few inmates had already risen. I walked towards the washroom with my toothbrush and paste, freshened up, and returned to the room. I was not in the mood to speak to anyone, let alone look at them.

I didn't have my mobile and didn't know how to contact Amma back home. The inmates of the hostel began approaching me one by one. Most of them were Indians, and they spoke to my daughter and me pleasantly, inquiring about why we were there. I briefly explained my husband's passing. At that moment, they reassured me that everything would be alright; they would not keep us there for long and would send us back to India.

Most of them had come here as domestic help. Their employers abused them, withheld their pay, and confiscated their passports. Due to the abuse, they often escaped to the nearest police station and ended up here in the hostel. I was surprised that some had been in the hostel for almost ten years! Yet, they seemed happy. They had resigned to their fate, accepting that they would likely never return to India and see their loved ones again. Back home, there was so much poverty; here, at least, their basic needs were met. No mobile phones were allowed, which meant they had no means of contacting their families, nor could they be certain that their families would accept them. They were provided with food and clothing, and life was relatively comfortable there.

I waited for two days, and nobody showed up for me. I almost gave up hope. I thought there was no way anyone could come and fetch me from this hostel. As I looked around, it appeared that nobody ever left this place once they arrived. Some of the women were elderly. What surprised me was how joyful they looked. Some of their family members might not even know they were alive. I didn't understand why the government was not sending them back to their families. What could be the reason or benefit of keeping them here?

The hostel took special care of me and my child. They regularly provided diapers and even brought her toys.

The wardens were kind. Once, the warden told me that they were not meant to keep my case here in the hostel. With a child in tow, the education of the child becomes their responsibility. Since the police brought us here; they had no other option.

The next day, I received a call on my mobile. They had kept it charged. Whenever we got a call, we were summoned to the reception to receive it. It was my brother-in-law again. He said he had contacted someone in Saudi Arabia through a contact from a town near my village. He mentioned that the person might come to the hostel and asked me to provide the address. I did not know the address, so I asked my brother-in-law to tell the gentleman to call me so the receptionist could guide him in Arabic.

I had lost all hope. I thought, "Who in their right mind would come to rescue me?"

On the third day, there was a call on the mobile again. The person on the other end introduced himself as "Sajid". To my surprise, he spoke to me in my mother tongue, *Tulu* [35]. He said he would come and meet me

---

35. Tulu: Language spoken mainly in the coastal district of Udupi and Mangalore of Karnataka State, India.

and asked for the address. I gave the phone to the warden, who guided him to the location.

This was perhaps the longest day of my life. I was waiting for Sajid every minute. He finally turned up at night, accompanied by the police.

A medium-height, lean-built man with a beard and glasses. He had a very unassuming personality, but he had an aura of friendliness. As women, we have this sixth sense for identifying threats in a person, no matter how well-behaved they may seem. With this gentleman, I found it particularly comforting.

Sajid looked me in the eye and then told me in Tulu, "These people will ask you if you know me. Please say yes, you know me and are willing to come with me."

I was unprepared for this. I felt a bit tense. How do I say I know him when I do not know who he is, and how do I go with him? I thought the hostel was safer. Yet, somehow, since childhood, despite our absolute poverty, I have never liked staying in anyone's house. Therefore, I was unwilling to go to another home, and God knows what awaited me there. I wanted to remain in this hostel or return to India. I desired only these two options. However, I also wished to keep my options open. He had anticipated my hesitation, I suppose. He went out and brought his wife and child along. Then he spoke to me in Tulu, "Please do not hesitate. We have to send you back to India. For that, you will need to cooperate. I cannot do anything with you sitting here." His wife also spoke to me, holding my hands. I could tell they were trying to put on a façade before the police as if they knew me well.

I felt a bit more at ease after speaking to his wife. I was willing to take a risk now. At least if I got out of this place, I should be able to contact someone. I agreed and then decided to go with them. The policeman asked me if I knew them. I replied yes. He then asked if I was willing to go with them. I said yes. I had to sign a register stating I was going of my own accord. I told Sajid I would pack my things and come.

The moment I went to my room and informed the other female residents that I was moving out, joy erupted around me. They were all so pleased for me and started cheering. They helped me pack my belongings in no time. They were genuinely thrilled for me. Although I had only been there for three days, we had formed a close bond. Saarika received hugs and kisses from all of them. They embraced me and bid me farewell.

Sajid then drove my daughter and me to his house, about 30 minutes from the hostel. Along the way, I left two voice messages for my mother and brother-in-law. If fate were to be believed, anything could go awry. They needed to know where I was heading if I could not contact them again.

The Desert's Unexpected Family

We arrived at Sajid's house and entered his modest home, where his wife, Aisha, invited me to freshen up. I was eager for a bath. After a long, refreshing soak for Saarika and me, I came out to find that we were to be served some Mangalorean-style fish curry and rice. It had been nearly two weeks since I had enjoyed a proper home-cooked meal.

Sajid sat across from me and asked if I felt comfortable recounting the entire story. I replied affirmatively and narrated the whole incident. Once I finished, Sajid informed me that there would be some formalities at the police station and that I would need to navigate the legal system of Saudi Arabia. He assured me of assistance with all the formalities for my daughter and me to return to India. I began to feel a sense of relief wash over me. I thought, God, let me return home to my mother.

Sajid, whom I began calling Sajid-*bhai*[36] said, "The cops may ask whether you want Sukesh's body to be sent back to India or buried here. What's your opinion?" I paused for a moment, recalling and responding, "He had converted to Islam, and he always expressed that he should be buried and not cremated. He was frightened of fire or burning. That was, I believe, his last wish. If I take his body to India, nobody will understand this final wish of his, and he will not be buried but cremated according to local traditions."

However, Sajid Bhai was sceptical. He said, "I doubt they will agree to his last wishes." He was also quite astonished by how much the *Kafeel*[37] believed in Sukesh. He remarked, "My Kafeel treats me like a servant, even though I am a Muslim. I'm astonished at how well they treated Sukesh. That speaks to how skilled Sukesh was in managing people. He must be a brilliant chap. Forget one person; five individuals have invested in him. That says a lot about him."

I reluctantly asked Sajid Bhai, "Who contacted you and told you about me? And why are you helping me?"

---

36. Bhai: Brother
37. Kafeel: A sponsor of the job of an outsider in Arabic.

To me, the answer to the latter part was very important, as I could not grasp why a stranger would go out of his way to assist a woman whose husband had been murdered. What was in it for him? Why would anyone do this without expecting some gain themselves?

"I got a call from the *Imam*[38] of *Kapu*[39]. Your brother-in-law is familiar to him, so he contacted me and told me about you. I conducted my search and discovered that you were staying in the hostel.

He continued, "I work for a private lighting company here and am part of an association of Indian expatriates established by the Indian Embassy, which assists individuals in need in Tabuk. We have unwell people who experience road accidents or suffer from workplace incidents. We, from the association, help these individuals through the Indian Embassy." However, yours is the first case that involves murder. As you know, crime is quite rare in this country. I felt bad that a mother and child had to live in a hostel for no fault of theirs. I confided in my wife, though she was honestly not very comfortable with it, as this involved a police investigation. But Allah guided me to you. Perhaps it

---

38. Imam: A Muslim preacher/leader
39. Kapu: Name of a place near Udupi

was due to the good deeds performed by your husband. Maybe." He shrugged his shoulders.

I was immune to such modesty owing to my experience with my late husband. Perhaps Sajid Bhai noticed this in my expression and continued, "You must believe me when I say I have no other mala-fide intentions. My mission is to assist you in leaving the hostel, which I have done. Next is to send you back to India. That's all. However, before that, we need to clear all the legal formalities here so you can safely fly back to India. Until then, you can stay at my house. It won't be long. Perhaps 2-3 weeks!"

I looked at him with intense, searching eyes, hoping to detect any hint of dishonesty that my alert radar might pick up by now. But no! His statement was honest; he meant what he said.

Sajid Bhai's house was a simple dwelling with one hall, three bedrooms, and a kitchen. They had made some partitions and converted one of the bedrooms into a separate living space with its entrance from the outside. One of Aisha's friends and her husband lived there temporarily.

Days passed by

Clothing was becoming a significant issue for me. Previously, it was just Sukesh and me, and I had all the T-shirts and pyjamas at home. I had to slip a burqa on top if I needed to go out. Who cared what one wore underneath? But I found it so challenging here, in a stranger's house. Poor Aisha bought me some dresses, and they vacated one of their bedrooms for Saarika and me to use.

For some reason, I wanted solace. I wished to be alone. I needed space. I wanted time to think. As someone was always around, I wasn't getting enough time for myself. I was yearning for solitude. However, Sajid Bhai encouraged me to feel comfortable. He advised me to stop worrying and to start contemplating how to face my future in India. Aisha's friend was about to leave because her visa was about to expire, so Sajid Bhai said, "If you wish, you can move in here. We shall write to the Indian embassy, and they will reimburse us for the rent and some expenses." He offered me an option. After two weeks, the tenants moved to India, and I began living there. I would often help Aisha in the kitchen.

They had two children. Their younger daughter was almost two years old, the same age as my daughter. Additionally, they had an older son who was six and exceptionally bright. I used to assist him with his homework. My daughter was very happy playing with their daughter, as she found a wonderful companion.

Identification

The next morning, being Friday and a weekly holiday, Sajid Bhai called me again to the living room.

"The authorities have called. They want you to identify Sukesh's body and sign some paperwork for the last rites to be performed." These matters don't stop, do they? I was not ready to look at his dead body. I wanted to remember him as he was—alive! I couldn't even bear the thought of seeing his lifeless form.

I replied, "I can't do that, Sajid Bhai. I can't bear to see him dead. That's not the way I wish to remember him. I want to hold onto the image of him as he always was— cheerful and smiling. I can't do this, please. You have already done so much for me. I beg you to do this one thing for me."

"Sister, I'm not authorised in your absence. You have endured so much. May this be the last time? Please gather your strength and do this for the final time. I believe he would find peace in it as well." His wife, Aisha, also joined in urging me to comply.

I wore my burqa and sat in Sajid Bhai's car. It was a small place compared to the usual large buildings in Saudi Arabia. Sajid Bhai was speaking to someone at the counter when he signalled to me. I walked up to him, and we were taken inside a large cold room with numerous cubicle steel doors along the wall. Each cubicle had a number and something else written in Arabic. This was a morgue. The attendant opened one of the cubicle doors. My heart was pounding so hard that I feared it might burst. He reached inside and pulled out a sliding steel plate. On it lay a dead body wrapped in white linen. I had only seen such a scene in films. I froze in place. I was not prepared for this. The attendant removed the linen from the dead body's face. For a moment, I was taken aback. I suddenly moved closer. It wasn't Sukesh. I edged even closer to observe. No, that was not him. This person appeared thin and frail. Could they have the wrong person? Was Sukesh alive? Had he managed to fool these people?

I told Sajid Bhai, "No, that's not him."

There was a puzzled look on his face. "Please check carefully again."

"No, that's not him."

Sajid Bhai informed the attendant of the same. Both were conversing in Arabic. The attendant stepped forward and then uncovered the cloth covering his waist. I could see that the corpse had a large birthmark on the right side, just below the chest. Yes, that was him. It was indeed him. He had been a chubby chap, and here I was, confronted with a frail face. What had torture, possible starvation, and two weeks in the freezer done to him? I broke down, sobbing, and rushed out of the room. I felt nauseous. I went into the lavatory and threw up.

Courtroom Odyssey

The two weeks were ending, as Sajid Bhai had promised. I was feeling restless. The time had come for me to go to the police station. Sajid Bhai informed me that the police would question my relationship with him and might regard us suspiciously. I would need to tell them that we were acquainted from our hometowns and that I was unaware that Sajid Bhai lived here. I had reached out to him through the Indian Embassy.

The following day, Sajid Bhai took me to the police station. They questioned me exactly as Sajid Bhai had anticipated. I answered precisely as I had been instructed. Sajid Bhai informed them that he was a member of the Indian Embassy Assistance Team and would oversee the entire case proceedings on my behalf from that point forward. They consented.

Fortunately, the court complex was directly opposite Sajid Bhai's house, allowing us to walk there easily. We only had to cross the wide road. The following day, we needed to attend court. It was a substantial building and did not resemble the typical courtrooms we see in India.

I had never been to a court in India either; my experience had been limited to viewing it from the outside, with the next best thing being what I had seen in movies. Inside, it appeared more like a corporate office.

Saarika and I were ushered into a waiting room designated for women. In addition to myself, an elderly lady was sitting there. We spent some time in the air-conditioned room when Sajid Bhai arrived at the door and called for me. We entered an adjoining room, approximately 1000 square feet in size. I could see the judge seated on a raised platform, wearing a Kaffiyeh. Alongside him were his assistant, my translator, and Sajid Bhai. The judge asked me to state my name through the translator. After a few general inquiries about myself, I was invited to narrate my version of events. I recounted everything as it happened. The judge listened intently, occasionally seeking clarification. He then communicated something to his assistant, who exited the chamber. I stood at a respectful distance from the judge.

A few policemen entered alongside Moosa and the other three individuals who were present at Moosa's house on the day I last met Sukesh. I was taken aback to see that they were shackled at both hands and feet, reminiscent of those scenes we used to watch in old

Hindi films. The judge instructed me to identify all of them. I glanced at Sajid Bhai's face.

The judge said, "Don't look anywhere else. Don't think that being an expat will exempt you from justice. Justice is the same for everyone here. Just as we endeavour to be fair with you, you should cooperate and be truthful. Tell us everything as it is. We expect that from you."

I felt a deep sadness as I looked at their faces through my Burqa. I didn't want to identify them. They appeared worn out. I could see their ghostly faces. They knew very well that if I recognised them and said yes, their lives would be ruined. Sajid Bhai had told me, "This is not the time to be compassionate. You should say yes or no if you have seen them with Sukesh on the last day you met him. This is not India. Don't try to be forgiving here. You may, in turn, end up in trouble." These cautionary words of Sajid Bhai before entering the court complex resonated in my mind.

I looked at them and told the judge that, apart from these four, there was one more person that day. I didn't want to contradict my earlier statement that I had said five people were in the room that day. The judge began shouting at them and asked who the other person was. Moosa and the others denied the existence of anyone else. I was certain there were five of them, including Moosa, apart from Aslam. The arguments continued back and forth between the judge, Moosa, and the others for quite some time.

Later, when we got home, I was utterly upset. I started crying. I told Sajid Bhai, "I can't go through this. I know Sukesh is dead. But there were mistakes on his part as well. Now, I cannot jeopardise the lives of these others. I cannot sacrifice another five to justify one." Sajid Bhai replied, "I can understand your feelings. But they are not innocent. They had no right to kill him."

Yet sometimes, I wonder if they actually killed him. They might have tortured him into confessing, but they may not have been the ones to end his life. Moosa, being a policeman, knew the consequences of killing in this country. He couldn't have been that foolish. Did Sukesh take his own life? Or did he suffer a heart attack or something? I may never know.

The court saga continued for several days. Poor Sajid Bhai would take me along whenever there was a court date. He usually had a half-day duty at his office. They also required a translator in court, from Arabic to Hindi. We had this Pakistani chap as my translator. The hearing would be postponed on any day when the translator did not show up.

The one person missing from the five was Moosa's elder brother. I later realised that they needed him to run errands on their behalf. That is why they had, somehow, kept him out of this. They thus argued that there were only four of them. Eventually, I understood what was happening and agreed in the court that there were only four of them and that I might have been mistaken. Immediately, the judge asked me if I was being coerced, threatened, or contacted by the accused. I replied no.

At one of the hearings, the judge asked me if I knew of Sukesh's last wishes. I responded that he wished to be buried here in Saudi Arabia. To this, the judge remarked, "We cannot bury a non-Muslim here. Mortal Remains of non-Muslim nationals can be buried only in earmarked non-Muslim cemeteries in few select cities or have to be sent back to their country of origin if you are willing to bear the cost."

Through the interpreter, I replied, "He converted to Islam a few years ago. I even have his last voice message, in which he mentioned that. If permitted, I can play it for you." Moosa interjected, saying, "Yes, it has been five years since he converted, and I took him to Dammam for the process." The judge asked me if I was aware that he had embraced Islam and that his Muslim name was Abdul Rehman. I nodded in the affirmative.

I had been wondering what had happened to Moosa's wife for days. One day during the hearing, Moosa's wife was brought to the court. I was informed that she, too, had been arrested, which surprised me. She was causing quite a commotion, and I could not understand what they were discussing. Unlike in India, they did not have lawyers here. We interacted directly with the judge. It seemed that she was pleading with the judge and was in tears. Sajid Bhai later told me that she had requested the judge to let her see her husband. The judge replied, "You did not allow the lady to speak to her late husband when she begged you. You, too, must undergo the same now." And they led her away. Once again, my womanly instinct kicked in. Poor thing, she had likely nothing to do with all of this. Why had they arrested her? She has such small children. When I told Sajid Bhai this, he said, "Why don't you request the judge? Let's see what the judge will say."

I told my translator to convey my message to the judge. He did so, and the judge said he would think it over.

Later, I learned that Moosa's wife was released the following day.

Life in Sajid Bhai's house

Sajid Bhai was a medium-built, bespectacled man with a moustache and beard, sporting typical South Indian features, such as a dusky complexion and dark eyelashes. He must be in his early 40s. I wouldn't describe him as a very conservative Muslim, but he did pray daily. I never saw him miss Friday prayers at the nearby mosque during my brief time with his family. He had a very pleasing personality and was quite soft-spoken. The children, including Saarika, enjoyed his company immensely. She looked forward to his return from work each evening, as he would bring toffees for his two kids, alongside Saarika. Both husband and wife were very cordial; in my short time with them, I never witnessed them being angry with each other. He was truly a Godsend for me.

Sajid Bhai was part of the local Indian diaspora assistance group. They had a good rapport with the India Passport and Application Centre in Tabuk and the Indian Embassy in Riyadh. Their group provided help to needy individuals. Sajid Bhai mentioned that this was the first time he had been involved in a murder case. He would often jest that in his 12 years of living in Saudi Arabia, he had never seen a police station, sat in a police vehicle, or entered a court, yet I had managed to experience all of this in my six months there. He wished to return to India in another year or so. The main reason Indians came to work here was the advantageous conversion rate to Indian rupees and the absence of personal income tax. He had booked a flat in Mangalore and hoped to return to India to start a business.

The man had taken an enormous risk in getting involved in my case. He told me on the first day that his wife, Aisha, was uncomfortable with his involvement. I, too, would have felt the same way had I been in her position. However, Sajid Bhai seems to have assured Aisha that this was a God-sent order and that He had chosen him for this noble work. He also told Aisha that had it been her instead of me, wouldn't she expect someone to assist her? That is how he had persuaded her to join him the day he came to the hostel to secure my release.

Aisha was a strikingly attractive, slender, fair lady, perhaps in her early 30s. There appeared to be a significant age difference between Sajid Bhai and her. While Sajid Bhai was soft-spoken, she could be described as 'Silent.' She was indeed very soft-spoken and timid. Not a single day did she make me feel unwanted or like an intruder. Who would wish to host a stranger, especially a woman with a child, in a highly conservative foreign country? I truly admire her empathy towards me. She would feed Saarika the same things as her children. Had she not cooperated, I wouldn't have managed all this alone. I never saw her quarrel with her husband, although the gentleman was busy balancing his job, my court appearances, and his family obligations.

Sajid Bhai would take me to court whenever there was a hearing. I could sense that Aisha, his wife, was feeling the pressure, and I completely related to her. Any woman, for that matter, would become frustrated when her husband gave so much importance and attention to a stranger woman. I was aware of these situations and ensured I was always on good terms with Aisha, which was very important. After all, I was merely a small blip in their lives. Once I returned, they would have to live together for the rest of their lives.

It was also crucial for me to provide clarity to Aisha. Therefore, I informed her at the outset not to harbour any doubts or ill will. My sole intention was to return to India with my daughter; I would not create any trouble for her or her family. Given my situation, Sajid Bhai was more than a brother to me, as I felt that even if I had a brother, he would think twice before helping given my situation. Consequently, Aisha was very friendly towards me. She never made me feel awkward, nor did I give her any reason to feel uncomfortable. I was exceedingly cautious.

I had drawn a clear boundary regarding my limits. I never left my room when Sajid Bhai was around unless I wanted clarification or he called me over to discuss the case. I always assisted Aisha with her household chores and kitchen work. I never switched on the TV by myself nor was I interested in it. I have never served food on my own. I was like a mouse scurrying about, constantly running back to my burrow at any opportunity.

I helped her children with their studies. Her son was bright, and her daughter was good friends with Saarika. Saarika also liked all of them. She called Sajid Bhai 'Abbu', as his children did, and Aisha 'Ammi'. As Saarika was hyperactive, she took liberties with them.

Sajid Bhai would invite my daughter and me whenever they went out. I would vehemently refuse, as I did not want to intrude on their privacy. I felt it was important to respect that, as I knew the consequences could be severe. At times, Aisha would request me to join, but I remained firm in my refusal. Saarika would accompany them, which I could not prevent, much to my helplessness.

Despite my utmost caution, one day, their son had a half-day at school, and Sajid Bhai, who usually picked him up, was delayed due to my court hearing. Preoccupied with the situation, he unintentionally forgot to pick up his son. The boy was due to be picked up at 12:30 pm, but on that day, it was 2:30 pm when we returned from the court. Halfway home, Sajid Bhai remembered that he hadn't picked up his son. He rushed to the school. Aisha was furious when they arrived home. She was also angry with me and didn't speak to me for a while. It was natural for her to feel that way. I apologised profusely. The only saving grace was that Saarika was very fond of her, and so was she. That's why I was spared that day. It was my mistake, too. I should've warned Sajid Bhai in time, but I forgot to.

There used to be daily visitors to Sajidbhai's house. The local Indian community would come to talk to me and try to extract gossip. Aisha and Sajid Bhai would become furious. Everyone knew about the situation, yet nobody stepped forward to help. Now, everyone was eager to come over and check on the juicy gossip.

I also wrote to the Indian Embassy almost daily, explaining my situation and requesting reimbursement for my rent along with some extra funds. Sajid Bhai assisted me with the writing. I had no money at all. These total strangers were looking after my daughter and me, and I felt I was burdening them. Therefore, I had to request money from the embassy to pass on to Sajid Bhai. After much correspondence, during which I had to explain everything anew each time, they began sending some money as rent reimbursement.

The Judgement Day

It has been almost four months now. I was becoming desperate. The legal system now resembled the Indian system to me. It was delayed for one reason or another. One fine day, the judge reserved the next hearing for judgement.

That day, I was a mixed bag of emotions. Aisha accompanied me to the court at my request, along with Sajid Bhai. We sat on one of the sofas positioned on either side of the room at the back. Moosa and three others were standing at the opposite end near the judge, facing him. They were in chains and prisoners' clothes. I noticed a few more people seated on the opposite sofa; I think one was Moosa's wife. There were several other men and women, at least 10 to 12 of them. There were only three of us.

My emotions were truly on a roller coaster. Why am I sitting here? What do I expect the judge to rule? Do I seek to avenge my husband's death? Is it justified to take four lives for one life lost? Won't these women be left as widows? Their children without a father, possibly a breadwinner? Will these women and their children curse me and my daughter? Is it justified? How is this justice? Will my husband's soul find peace? Does something called a soul even exist?

Was it an intentional murder? Are they murderers? Haven't they tortured and killed my husband? I did see the torture marks on his body. Should I be vengeful because of this? But strangely, I was not. Why wasn't I? Do I forgive them? Will that be justice? Justice for me, Saarika, and Sukesh? I heard they beheaded them publicly. I did my research on YouTube. Oh, God. It would be so gruesome. Imagine their family members receiving the beheaded corpses. I had tears in my eyes when the loud voice of the judge interrupted my wandering thoughts. The judge was reading something and looking at the accused intermittently. After about five minutes of reading, the women in the group who had come on behalf of the accused suddenly began wailing. The men stood and prayed, looking up. I knew at that instant that something terrible had been pronounced.

I glanced at Sajid Bhai. He extended his hand towards me, gesturing for me to remain silent as he tried to hear what the judge had to say. By this time, the police had arrived and asked the wailing women to leave the courtroom. After the judge had finished, I saw the four men standing in chains. They all had turned towards their family members, gazing at them with such sorrowful expressions. Moosa locked his eyes onto mine for a moment before looking towards the women huddled in burqas. I was wearing a burqa, too. Yet, I could feel his helpless gaze piercing through it, conveying something unspoken. What was he trying to say?

"Hope you are satisfied with the pronouncement." Or was it,

"So, you got justice?"

Perhaps, "Do you think this is justice? And what your husband did to us—what was that?"

Or maybe, "I am sorry for all that has happened."

I have no idea what it was. But my head was aching by now. Sajid Bhai bent towards me and said, "They have been awarded four years of imprisonment and, post that, execution by beheading. All four of them were found guilty." I felt a drop of sweat running down my forehead towards my cheeks, even in this air-conditioned hall.

Did I feel good about it? Honestly, no!

Setting aside the local judiciary, my mind acted as the judge by weighing the options. For starters, the Moosa I knew was a genuinely good man. Sukesh and he shared a particularly special relationship. Sukesh, his wife, and his child survived because of this man's generosity. They invested money in Sukesh due to their confidence in him. How Sukesh lost all the money remains a mystery to me, as I was not privy to those details. Did they have the right to be furious with Sukesh? Yes, of course, who wouldn't be? Did they have the right to kill him? Absolutely not. I do not know the circumstances surrounding his death. Was it due to their torture or something else?

Did Sukesh deserve to die like this? Of course not. Nobody deserves to be treated this way, least of all Sukesh. Did Sukesh cheat them? I am unaware of the circumstances, so I cannot pass judgment. However, Sukesh did confess to me that there was a misappropriation of funds he had borrowed from them and that he could not repay them. He did not inform me what he did with the money or how much money was involved. He had told me that the less I know, the better it is. Now, I understand the seriousness of those words.

I wondered, is justice served by condemning to death the people who allegedly killed Sukesh? This was the difficult part. I have nothing against these four individuals, particularly Moosa. Will I get Sukesh back by killing these four in retaliation? No. Then what is justice? Will I feel glad that the killers of my husband are to be executed? Again… I don't know. What is there to celebrate about taking a life? The killing of Sukesh may not have been intentional. Given the stringent laws of this land, these individuals must have known the consequences they faced. Mainly, Moosa, being a police officer, surely knew he would be facing severe penalties if he killed Sukesh. So, how did Sukesh die? Again, I have no idea.

My life has been a roller coaster since I married Sukesh. Was he an evil man? No! Not at all. He was a kind, loving, and compassionate individual. He never abused me or treated me poorly. He enjoyed pampering me. He was such a wonderful father to Saarika. He was very much attached to me and never intended for me to experience pain.

However, his poor financial discipline made him a trouble magnet. What was I seeking from this justice system? I questioned myself. Honestly, I didn't care. All I wanted now was to return to India with my daughter ASAP—immediately—on the first flight I could manage to get on. Nothing else mattered to me now. I had had enough of this.

The thoughts crashed over me like ocean waves during high tide—only, these were tides of the desert. Coming out of the court, I asked Sajid Bhai, "Is it done? What's next? When can I return to India? How do I go? Will the Embassy assist me financially? What about my Visa?" Our Visas had expired. I was unaware of the procedure for this. I would once again be at the mercy of Sajid Bhai for that.

Sajid Bhai replied, "One thing at a time. There will be a few more formalities in court, particularly regarding your compensation. The court may direct some compensation to be awarded to you. Once that is sorted, we shall contact the Indian Embassy and arrange for your exit through diplomatic channels. Even I am not entirely sure how it works."

My mind, meanwhile, was half relieved and half tense. I was relieved that the legal process was complete, but I was tense as I was still in Saudi Arabia and unsure how and when I would return to India.

The Dilemma

After two restless days, Sajid Bhai called me into the living room that evening. His wife, Aisha, was also present.

Sajid Bhai said, "The brother-in-law of Moosa contacted me today."

My heart sank. I was not prepared for this. I thought everything was over. I desperately wished to leave this country and return to my quaint little village.

"They are offering Diya."

"What's that?"

"Diya, in Islamic law, is the financial compensation paid to the victim or the heirs of a victim in cases of murder. In English, it's called Blood Money, akin to the Hindi word 'Daya,' which means mercy."

"Why are they offering it?"

"You must pardon Moosa and the others for their crime before the court in exchange for the money. That is if you are willing. There is no obligation on you."

"What?" I had never heard anything like this before, not in my country. I stared at him blankly, noticing that Sajid Bhai was shifting uneasily on the sofa he occupied.

"So, you mean I take money and pardon them? And they will be released?"

"Yes."

"What should I say to Sukesh? What should I say to my conscience? What should I tell his parents?"

"What should I tell Saarika when she grows up? That I took the money and pardoned her pappa's killers?" I exclaimed without thinking and then fell silent. A hush fell over the room.

I looked at Sajid Bhai and said, "You know how small the village where I live is. How do you think people will receive me back home?" Sajid Bhai was sitting with his arms folded over his chest, gazing down at the floor, deep in thought. After a pause, I said in a feeble voice, "I may forgive them, Sajid Bhai. But not in exchange for money. That would be a disgrace to Sukesh."

I continued, "I've already found a job back home in Udupi. I'll manage to survive somehow. I have a house to live in. I have a purpose for my daughter to live for. I'll figure out how to make ends meet." I glanced at Aisha. She was silent but was looking at me. I turned to Sajid Bhai once more.

Finally, he broke his silence. "Sister, let's think this over. There's no hurry. We can discuss this further. Though I lack in-depth knowledge on the subject, I do know that such a system exists in this part of the world." With that, he stood up and walked away.

Just when I thought everything had settled and there wouldn't be any more surprises, life dragged me by the hair and threw me back into the Colosseum, saying, "I'm not done with you yet! Fight…!" Here I was, like an injured gladiator, unwilling to give up, rising from the ashes, bruised all over, with the last ounce of strength remaining, standing up once more to face the wrath.

I couldn't sleep the whole night.

The following morning, at breakfast, Aisha summoned me into the living room. An eerie silence filled the room. Shifting uneasily on the sofa, Sajid Bhai began in a low voice, saying, "Sister, I understand your emotional turmoil. Coming from the same place as you, I am also aware of society's mindset. However, for a moment, let's set all that aside. You mentioned that you have loans to repay, specifically those related to your marriage. You have also indicated that your financial situation back home is poor. You have a daughter to raise. Her education, her marriage, your healthcare, and your ageing mother's healthcare all present significant financial challenges for you."

"I do not wish to undermine your determination to face these challenges; please don't misconstrue my intent. If I were in your situation, I would think similarly. However, let me explain why I am asking you to take a step back and reflect."

"You have consistently expressed sympathy for those four men. You never wanted them to receive a death sentence in the first place. You see, that's the crux of the matter. In numerous cases, the victim's family harbours such resentment against the killers that the notion of pardon would never even cross their minds."

"On the contrary, there was a case a few months ago in which the mother of the victim pardoned her son's murderer, who was his childhood friend, at the last minute, with the noose still around his neck. She slapped him on the face and forgave him as both families broke

down in tears. That's the legal system of this country."
Sajid Bhai took a long pause, and judging by my body
language, I was unconvinced. He took a deep breath
and continued, "Think about it with a calm mind."

"I urge you to think practically. I'm not certain that this
is the right course of action. Let's conduct a fact check.
Sukesh is gone. Nothing can or will bring him back. Do
you agree?"

I nodded my head.

"Set aside all societal judgements. You never wished
for Moosa and the others to be killed as retribution."

"Your financial situation is poor."

I sat there, absorbing every word that emanated from
Sajid Bhai's mouth.

"You didn't have much choice regarding this in your
life. Now, you have three options."

> *"First, Moosa and the others shall not be
> pardoned; they will then be beheaded, and
> you will return to India empty-handed with
> your daughter. "*

"Secondly, you pardon Moosa and others and spare their lives, yet refrain from accepting any money from them due to the fear of society's judgement."

"Thirdly, you forgive them while accepting a reasonable sum of money they can afford, ensuring that both your life and your daughter's are secure."

"The choice is yours. I don't want to hear anything right now. I'm not influencing you into any decision. I want you to be very practical about your thoughts without worrying about what society around you has to say. The same society you are concerned about may not be of much help when you are struggling to make ends meet once you return. Yes, there will be loose talk. Either way, they talk. Which is better? They talk about you having an empty pocket, or they talk about you having a healthy bank balance?"

"I have also come from a poor background with a large family of eight to support. My father was a fisherman who would somehow make ends meet. Many days, we went hungry as we had no agricultural land. Food had to be purchased. No catch, no food. I clearly understand the importance of money in human life. People may preach that money doesn't buy happiness. But all those preachers are the ones with truckloads of money. I disagree with them and am sure you would too. Money may not be everything, but it is almost everything. So, sister, please sleep over it. Take your time and make a very conscious decision."

I was unaware that this formed part of a larger negotiation in these countries. The victim and his family could be granted a pardon if the perpetrator's family provides sufficient money. Should I pardon these individuals? And that, too, in exchange for money? How morally justifiable is that? What would people back home think of me? Can I truly place a value on my husband's life?

I gave it considerable thought. I spoke to Amma. She didn't know what to say. She urged me to do what I felt was right but to return home soon. She was more concerned about our coming back home. Yet, being the practical woman she was, she added, "What life has taken away from you or your daughter cannot be regained. That was destiny. However, if you can secure your daughter's future by accepting the compensation, I don't think there is any harm in pardoning them. You not only save four lives; you also have something to fall back on when you return. It is a means to get your life back on track."

I mulled over it for two days. Practically, morally, and emotionally. It seemed pragmatic that I could get my life back on track with some money. But no amount of money could bring Sukesh back. I didn't want four more lives to be lost, with or without money. I didn't wish to be the reason for those lost lives. How was that justice? Four lives for one? I had a strong sense that Moosa couldn't have murdered him. I was thinking of Moosa's wife and his small children. One of his kids had become very attached to me towards the end of my stay at his home.

What would society say once I returned home? My village folks, Sukesh's parents, siblings, etc. Would they ridicule me for trading Sukesh's life for money? But I didn't kill him. Nor did he end up in that situation because of me. Should I pardon them without compensation? Was that wise of me?

I had a throbbing headache. I felt indecisive. Sajid Bhai was considerably older than I was. He hailed from my home district and knew the society in which I lived very well. Eventually, I thought that I should heed his advice. He was the one who brought me back from the brink. I could trust him completely. Whatever his decision, it was better for me to abide by it.

For some reason, that night, I slept exceptionally well. Perhaps when one is relieved of the burden of decision-making, the mind finds peace. I woke up early the next morning and still had very few thoughts. As I crossed the living room, I saw Sajid Bhai sitting on the sofa, sipping tea.

"Sajid Bhai, I will go with whatever you suggest. My daughter and I owe our lives to you. All your decisions for us thus far have turned out well. Even now, without much thought, I will follow your lead." I then walked towards the washroom.

The Art of Negotiating

"They have asked us to come to one of the mediator's offices. Let's go there and see how this goes. Even I am not very sure about this. I don't have anyone in my friend circle who has experience in this because crime is rare in this country. I'll ask some friends to join in." said Sajid Bhai.

"I spoke to some of my local Arab friends. They say you should demand 10 lakh Riyals. So that's the benchmark for negotiation."

Yes, just like you, I Googled the exchange rate. The exchange rate was around ₹15 per Riyal then. That amounted to ₹1.5 Crores! I rubbed my eyes again. I had to count the zeroes again to ensure I saw the right figure. This was beyond my imagination.

Off we went. Sajid Bhai, his two friends and myself.

I do not remember the exact location. It was a relatively small office space, and when we arrived, it was crowded with people. All were male. One person sat in an executive chair behind a large desk. Multi-seater sofas surrounded the room, all occupied by individuals mostly wearing thawbs. We took one side of a couch while I was given a separate chair. This was the advantage of wearing a burqa; it provided a sense of security. Negotiations commenced, and Sajid Bhai asked me in Hindi if I would pardon the accused if offered Diya.

I had already been tutored on what and how to respond, so I nodded in agreement. Then he inquired how much I desired for myself and my daughter to settle in life. I stated 10 lakh Riyals. After that, I became merely a mute spectator. Animated discussions unfolded in Arabic, which I understood nothing of, but I could sense the tension in the room. I wanted to grasp the subject of their conversation. Observing their body language, I could tell the opposing team seemed quite unhappy, while our side remained relentless.

I might be boring you with the same thoughts, but I wondered, what was I doing? Was I doing the right thing? Was I being selfish? I tried to block out all these thoughts. As I had decided earlier, I wanted to go with whatever Sajid Bhai chose. When Sajid Bhai stood up, it indicated to me that it was time to leave, but it seemed inconclusive to me.

On our way back, Sajid Bhai explained, "Sister, they said our demands are too high. Your husband has already placed them in a position of significant loss. They say they rarely trust outsiders. However, in your husband's case, they had placed great faith while investing. He has cheated them out of substantial sums of money. To gather that kind of money again would be difficult for them. They were requesting us to reconsider and asking us to show some mercy. But my friends maintain that these are part of the negotiations. They say that the other party will portray themselves as victims but are urging us to stand firm."

To be honest, my thoughts were aligned with theirs. I felt confused. After returning home, I confided in Sajid Bhai, stating, "I'm tired of this, Sajid Bhai. I want to return to India with my daughter. Let's not prolong this any further. I'm uncomfortable subjecting them to more hardships. I am also wasting your precious time."

The second round of meetings was arranged for a week later. On that day, an even more significant number of people had gathered. Aisha accompanied me, as I had requested her to join me. As instructed, I mentioned 10 lakh Riyals once again. Negotiations ensued once more. They continued for so long that we had three rounds of tea and one lunch round.

Ultimately, both parties agreed on 8 lakh Riyals in the end. Sajid Bhai had already informed me during the lunch break that if he were to ask me whether it was acceptable, I was to respond affirmatively. That was my cue. Accordingly, Sajid Bhai turned to me and asked if 8 lakh Riyals was acceptable. I hesitated. I can't recall what happened next. My mind went blank. I was observing them, and they were observing me. There was a hushed silence in the room. Those few seconds felt like an eternity. "Sister…" that was Sajid Bhai's voice. I came out of my stupor.

"Yeah?"

"Yeah… Okay!" I replied timidly.

Suddenly, a sigh of relief swept over the entire room. Everyone appeared relieved; I could see it. They embraced, holding one another's hands, some offering a small prayer while many expressed gratitude by saying, "Allah-hu-Akbar". I realised the gravity of the situation. At that moment, I felt I was doing the right thing. I felt vindicated from the guilt that had plagued me for days. Humans share the same emotions across geography, culture, religion, and creed. Though I couldn't comprehend a single word they were saying, I could certainly grasp the emotion behind the entire episode. I suddenly felt a tremendous weight lift off me. More than the money, the sensation of saving four lives from certain death was an immensely liberating experience.

The following day, we were summoned to the court to speak before the judge regarding the pardon. I asked Aisha, Sajid Bhai's wife, to accompany me. I approached the judge and conveyed my intentions.

The judge didn't seem surprised and said, "You need to demand 8 lakh Riyals from each of the four culprits. Don't be under any pressure. Being from another country doesn't mean you will not get justice here. You have to stick to your grounds."

I did not know what to reply. Am I supposed to follow the judge's instructions? Will it be treated as contempt if I disagree with the judge and stick to my ground?

Somehow, I was not convinced to ask for that kind of money. I did not want this to be a negotiating point in somebody's life. They, too, had lost money because of Sukesh. Over and above that, they had to collect money now, possibly. It was not easy to collect so much money. I was not in a state to demand more money from them. I was not willing to trouble them further. I thought this was quite a substantial amount for them to get. I was not willing to take advantage of the situation to the extent that I dried them out.

I mustered the courage and informed the translator that I would only adhere to the negotiated amount of 8 Lakh Riyals. The judge glanced towards me. With my burqa on, I had no idea what he was trying to judge. However, I had locked my gaze of determination upon him. It seemed he was attempting to ascertain whether I was under undue pressure.

"Is this your final decision? I hope you have thought this through carefully. Will the money reach you safely, or will it be given to someone here with you?"

"You are not under any pressure from anyone, are you? I trust you understand that you cannot appeal again once we conclude the case. Nor can you return to India and reopen the case. I will grant you a week, if necessary, to reconsider."

I replied immediately, "No, sir, I don't want more time. I've thought about it enough. Please release them."

The judge glanced at me intently for a moment. Then, as he turned to make a note in his records, he said, "It doesn't work like that here, lady. They have committed a crime that cannot be pardoned. You have pardoned them and granted them life. However, the law requires that they be punished for their misdeeds. Therefore, their four years of imprisonment stands."

Meanwhile, they were instructed to give the money to me before the judge. Moosa's elder brother then stated that they had arranged 4 lakh Riyals for the moment and requested a month for the remainder. My heart sank. Another month? No chance!

"When you committed to the money, you should have known!" exclaimed the judge. "It would be unjust to the lady and her child to delay after all they have endured. They need to return to India. I will give you one week. We shall reconvene next Wednesday. Ensure the remaining amount is arranged by then to settle this. Madam, please count the money and inform me if there are 4 lakh Riyals present," thundered the judge, disapproving of their request.

I slowly opened the envelope. I had no idea about the local currency. I glanced at Sajid Bhai, who then came over to help count. We counted the bundles, and Sajidbhai said it was fine. We walked out of the court together. Aisha was with me, and Sajid Bhai joined us as well. Meanwhile, Sajid Bhai had made all the arrangements for the money transfer. He had spoken to the branch manager of my bank back home regarding the situation unfolding here. I was unfamiliar with these money remittances. I had never seen so much money in my life. Comprehending these figures was far too much for me. Just then, Moosa's brother called us from behind. He told me directly in Arabic that I should deposit the money in the bank soon, as it was not safe to hold it in hand. Sajid Bhai translated that for me and assured him we would go to the bank to make the deposit.

Seriously? This place is the safest I've ever felt. He asked which bank it was, and Sajid Bhai told him. He offered to drop us off, but Sajid Bhai explained that we had a car and would drive ourselves. Sajid Bhai, his wife Aisha, and I drove to the location of the bank. Sajid Bhai noticed through the rearview mirror that we were being followed. I turned around and saw a white Toyota driven by Moosa's brother. Sajid Bhai chuckled and said, "They're probably worried that I might take a cut from you or rob you of the money. They're not wrong to think that."

When we arrived at the bank premises, they, too, parked their car next to ours and spoke to Sajid Bhai cordially. I did not inquire about what it was regarding.

This one was a women-only branch, with all staff and customers being women. Only Aisha and I could enter the bank. The officer behind the desk was taken aback when I mentioned the amount. She rose from her seat and entered a cabin, presumably occupied by the bank manager. The lady in the cabin approached us and asked a few questions regarding the source of the money. We explained everything to her, but she was unwilling to accept the cash. We tried to convince her, but she kept returning to her cabin to call someone, then come back to us for more details or to refuse the remittance. We stepped outside to inform Sajid Bhai when we spotted Moosa's brother standing there with him. We told both of them what had transpired inside. The men could not enter to persuade the lady manager. Meanwhile, Moosa's brother contacted someone and asked us to follow him. We returned to the court and waited inside the building. After half an hour, he emerged with a letter in Arabic that appeared to be an official court document. He asked us to present this letter to the bank manager, after which she would be obliged to assist us.

We returned and handed the letter to the manager. She made several more phone calls and ultimately agreed to accept the cash. You see, nothing happens to me in one go. The term seamless doesn't apply to me. There seem to be obstacles at every stage of my life. Every small, bloody step! The money was deposited equally into my mother's and my accounts.

From Arid Sands to Coastal Shores

I was feeling restless. I wanted to return home to see my mother. How much longer could I stay here?

Meanwhile, I wondered why Sajid Bhai was helping me so much. What was I to him? He hadn't given me even the smallest hint that he wanted a share of the money I received. Even if he had asked, I would have willingly given him the entirety. Who in their right mind would want a complete stranger, especially a woman with a child, in a foreign land, amid stringent laws, entangled in a murder accusation, to stay in their home? Even if he did, how did his wife Aisha agree to it? For all I know, Sajid Bhai was unaware I would receive a substantial sum leading to such circumstances. Initially, he had mentioned that I might claim compensation of a lakh or two Indian rupees. Money had never been a factor between us. He was purely a humanitarian. He is a Muslim, and I'm a Hindu. Back home, people of both our religions fight each other. There are riots and arson. They kill one another. Look at what happens when we find ourselves in a different country. We are united. We are cordial. We transcend religion, caste, creed, and gender when helping one another. Even Sukesh was extreme in his willingness to assist others. I suddenly recalled his words: *"All this help that I offer to people will return to you and our daughter as good karma."* Perhaps that's what drew Sajid Bhai to me.

Somehow, a week passed. Wednesday felt further away than ever. Sajid Bhai took me to court in the morning, and Aisha came along. Moosa's brother handed over the balance of 4 lakh Riyals while profusely saying something in Arabic. I interpreted it as him thanking me for saving his brother's and his friends' lives. The matter was settled. The judge issued the relevant orders, and we were given a copy. On the way to the bank to deposit the money, Moosa's brother was not with us this time. I felt a strong urge to share some money with Sajid Bhai for all the trouble he had taken for no apparent reason, but I wasn't sure how he would react. I knew he had booked a flat in Mangalore, India, and thought I could part with some money to help him. I set aside 1.5 lakh Riyals in cash and deposited the rest into my account. Aisha was seated in the waiting area and didn't notice how much I had deposited since the transaction went smoothly this time, thanks to the bank manager's cooperation.

Meanwhile, our expired visas had to be reinstated on special grounds, for which the court order copy was crucial. Once again leveraging his contacts, Sajid Bhai made the necessary arrangements for our visa renewals and tickets back to Mangalore via a connecting flight to Dubai. When Sajid Bhai handed me the physical ticket, tears welled up in my eyes once more. I had navigated so many uncertainties and twists in life that I was unsure this was the final hurdle. I felt extremely apprehensive. My state of mind was such that I was almost expecting something unfortunate to occur at any moment, whether in the next hour or day. The ticket was for the upcoming Saturday—just another four days. Sajid Bhai suggested I do some shopping, knowing I would not be returning. However, I was more eager to get home than to shop. I was aware that my family back home was looking forward to Saarika and me returning safely rather than me bringing them any gifts. Nevertheless, I accompanied him and Aisha. I bought a few toys for Saarika and Sajid Bhai's children, but that was all. I couldn't convince myself to purchase anything for myself.

Finally, the day of our departure arrived. It was time for us to fly back from the desert. I had mixed feelings. Everything I went through in the last nine months! It was such a roller coaster ride. Was I happy to go back?

Oh yes, I was. But I was also sad to leave behind Sukesh, resting six feet under. He was such a lovely human being. Unfortunately, he tended to get into trouble, which meant I also had to endure hardships. He would be alive today if all had been well, and we would have been happy together. Saarika would have had a father.

Sajid Bhai and his family have been angels sent from above. What else could I call them? They just appeared from nowhere at the remand home. I was leaving Saudi Arabia for good. I hugged Aisha tightly at the airport and touched Sajid Bhai's feet. Finally, I walked towards the check-in counter. We had to change flights in Dubai. But my mind was back home. After a 1.5-hour layover in Dubai, we were headed back to Mangalore. As we approached Mangalore Airport, the flight began to descend and the seatbelt signs illuminated. So far, so good—I chuckled, my eyes welling with tears. Looking out of the window, I spotted dense clouds below. It was the monsoon season in Mangalore, and we usually experience heavy rain here. The pilot announced turbulence, and the plane began to shake violently. I thought to myself, there you go, another twist in my life? Am I going to die? Will I never see Amma again? This sequence of thoughts raced through my mind, and

I hugged Saarika tightly, closing my eyes. I opened my eyes to the thud of the wheels touching the tarmac. Thank God! Finally!

I had already informed Amma about my landing time. I had asked her to hire a car from a local taxi service to come to Mangalore. I was not patient enough to wait another two hours before seeing Amma. I hurriedly walked out of the airport and spotted Amma's familiar smiling, glowing face. Wearing a maroon saree with a bindi on her forehead, her hair well-oiled and neatly tied into a bun, she stood there, tall, straight, with her arms crossed. To me, she looked like a goddess. I left my trolley halfway and ran to her with Saarika in my arms. My younger sister had also come and promptly took Saarika. I hugged Amma and began to cry. My stomach felt locked or cramped. For the second time, I struggled to breathe. The dam of my emotions burst forth. Amma held me close. I rested my head against her bosom.

Just then, my phone rang. It was Sajid Bhai. I beamed with joy and told him I had arrived safely. I thanked him and Aisha profusely.

Sajid Bhai said, "Thank God, you made it home safely. My contribution was small in the grand scheme of

God's will. But, sister, why did you leave that much cash at home? I read the accompanying letter and don't believe I deserve that money. When I come to Mangalore, I will return it. I cannot keep that money; that would not be right. It goes against God's will. Believe me, I can manage on my own. Blood money should only be with the rightful relatives. A third party cannot possess it, even if you will it."

It's been five years now. You must be wondering what I did with the money. I gave a small portion to my father-in-law. He was an old man, and so was his wife. They needed some cash for themselves at this age. After all, it was their son's blood money. I had considerable loans of my own and those of Sukesh to repay, and I cleared all of them. A few relatives discovered this and sought some money, which I could not refuse. I had to give some to my aunt, who took care of me selflessly during my time of need in Davangere.

Sajid Bhai returned the money I left for him in his drawer when he visited India. I built my mother's dream of an RCC-roofed house for us next to the existing thatched-roof house. I enrolled in a Bachelor's Degree in Medical Laboratory Technology at Manipal to keep my mind occupied and not dwell on all the unpleasant incidents I had experienced. I deposited the remaining money for the future. I have joined a reputable lab for experience, but I shall open my own lab soon. Saarika has been admitted to a good school. I live with my Amma, who is urging me to remarry. However, I believe I have had enough of it. I don't wish to marry again. What I have gone through in life has scarred me deeply. Marriage is frightening to me. I may find the right person someday if it is God's will. For now, life is wonderful.

Sorry… my name? You've gone through so many pages without discovering my name. You've experienced the emotions as I would have. So now, what's in a name?

The End